I0662383

The Lady from Toledo

A novel by

Tom Creary

Copyright 2014©Thomas Creary

All rights reserved

ISBN: 978 099 215 2017

Other novels by Tom Creary

The Bohemian Connection (2013)

The Russian Intrusion (2016)

Survivor (2017)

Sisters (2018)

To all my friends and memories of Africa

Preface

The story in this book is fiction, although inspired by a true story from a different time and another country. The places are real but the people and happenings in them are not.

I wish to thank Michèle Thinel, a fine and wise teacher of writing, for reviewing my writing of this story. She made it readable.

Tom Creary

April 2019

PART ONE

1

Columbus, Ohio

Jennifer Sutton, Jenny to everyone who knew her, didn't care what they thought. She was in love.

Things went so fast. They had met in the campus bookstore. He invited her for coffee, she invited him to an off campus yard party. They continued to see each other. They made love for the first time a month later.

He was 24. She was 20. He was studying to be a veterinarian and she was majoring in communications. He was from Yendi, Ghana. She was from Toledo, Ohio.

He was her African Apollo, the man of her life. And she didn't care that he was black.

Jenny and Sahr Akala were married in the summer of 1972. Although his family was Muslim, he had told Jenny and her parents that neither he nor his family were particularly devout. He had not objected to the Catholic wedding. They made for an impressive couple - he at six two and she tall as well at five ten. Jenny was slim of figure, had long dark brown hair, a beautiful face with large brown eyes and a pale complexion. This contrasted with Sahr's dark, handsomely refined features that could have come from a North African or Ethiopian connection somewhere in his family's lineage.

Jenny had introduced Sahr to her parents the previous Christmas vacation in Toledo. They came to appreciate the polite young man who their daughter was clearly in love with. Jim Sutton was a family doctor with an urban Toledo clientele and had many African-Americans as patients, but he had never thought his daughter would date one, much less marry one, although Sahr was not African-American. He was African. Jenny's mother was a pushover for the young man, who was polite and gracious with his bride's family, exhibiting an engaging sense of humor once the formalities of initial conversation were done with. She liked him right from the start. She was, however, worried that her youngest daughter would eventually be far from home, not fully believing Sahr's intention of remaining in the United States to practice as a veterinarian. In time, her intuition would be proven to be right. The Suttons had three other children, all older, but had lost their only son a few years before. James Sutton Jr. was a Naval Academy graduate and Navy pilot who was shot down during a raid over North Vietnam in the fall of 1968. Neither his body nor any trace of him or his plane had ever been found. He was presumed dead. Jim Jr. had left a widow with two young children in San Diego who the Suttons rarely saw since the death of their son. Their two other daughters were married, living in Connecticut and Maryland and raising young families.

Jenny graduated the spring after the wedding and went to work for a Columbus advertising agency, while Sahr still had two years to go in his four year program. Jenny became pregnant after a year on the job, but stayed with the firm until the birth of her daughter and went back to work a few weeks later. Jenny's mother spent a lot of time in Columbus that first year, looking after the baby as much as she could while Jenny worked and Sahr finished his studies. Soon after receiving his degree at the end of that year, he was hired by a country vet in a small town not far from Marion. He became a specialist in treating dairy cattle, travelling the back roads of farm country, helping with birthing and the treatment of sick calves. He was the first to say that he had become 'somewhat of an American.' With Jenny's assistance, he had become more comfortable in his adopted homeland. He and Jenny's parents had a good, easy relationship. Jim Sutton would take Sahr deer hunting with him in season as well as football games in the fall. The years in Ohio with another little girl born two and a half years after the first, were the best years of their time together. They loved each other and made for a handsome couple, the only mixed race one in that rural community. The prospect of returning home was not at the forefront of Sahr's mind, despite the occasional entreaties sent by his father asking him to return, and the admission to Jenny early in their marriage that someday he would feel compelled to do so. They tried not to talk or even think about it.

Sahr's family was prominent in Ghana. His parents were from different tribes inhabiting the north of the country. According to Ghanaian standards, the family was wealthy, part of the ruling class. Sahr's father was an entrepreneur in construction while his mother's family was active politically. An uncle had been one of the country's first ministers of foreign affairs after independence from Great Britain in the late 50's. Although Ghana was more Christian than Muslim, the Akala family was Muslim and had mildly expressed their disapproval of Sahr's marriage in a Catholic church, despite Sahr's assurances to the Sutton family of the contrary. This did not dampen their enthusiasm that their son would soon have children, though, and hopefully there would be sons who would do honor to the family. They had always taken it for granted that Sahr would return home after his studies to set up a veterinary practice in the area where they lived. He would be the first western-trained veterinarian in the Yendi area, and they were impatient with their son's reluctance to fulfill their designs for this to come about. Sahr was reminded of this occasionally in letters from home as he strove to learn the trade and look after his family. He had a good excuse for staying away, though. The politicians in his family were out of power at that time, with the fortunes of the Akala family much constrained because of it. Business was not good for Akala senior. Rivals aligned with the people in power were being favored for government business. It was all going their way. This could change. It was convenient, however, for Sahr to invoke the difficulties he would have in setting up a practice in the area that was controlled by the family of the Governor and a rival of the politicians in the extended Akala family.

One day in the late spring of 1977, Sahr Akala arrived home and announced to his wife that he was taking the family to Ghana. "It is time I returned, Jenny. To repay my parents and serve my people."

This was not really a surprise to her. They had spoken a few times of the inevitability of it ever since their engagement years before, although there had been little talk of it recently. She of course knew of the pressures he received from his family. Jenny looked her husband in the eye and could see he was serious. She had learned to recognize when her man had made a decision.

"It has been inevitable, Jenny. I have tried not to think of it for years. I love you. I have been happy here. But it is not home. I have recognized my calling."

"Why now, Sahr? What happened?"

"My mother called me at the clinic yesterday. She said that my father is sick. They don't know what he has, but he is not well. She asked me to come home. She said it was time, that she wanted to see her grandchildren, see them grow up. I have spent the last 24 hours thinking about it. I didn't sleep very well last night." Sahr was uncomfortable. He knew this would upset Jenny. But he had always known it would come to this. "Jenny, I am sorry. I will do the best I can to make a good life for you in my country, with my people. I hope you can believe me."

Jenny put her arms around her man and, with tears in her eyes, said "I understand. You are my man. I don't want to lose you. Give me time to get used to it. Please."

Jenny wiped her eyes and walked out the back door to sit in the yard. The girls were playing next door with the neighbor's children. Sahr followed her, sat down and took her hand in his. "We don't have to do this next week, Jenny. I told my mother I would let her know if and when we return. Let's think about it and then decide on timing."

Jenny was silent for a moment, then turned to Sahr. "Your father is sick. If we are to do this, let's get going on it," she replied, coming to grips with the reality of the move of her young family to Africa. She kissed her husband, took his hand, and led him back to the house where she took him to the bedroom. In the time they had been together, making love had taken care of pressures, arguments and emotional times, and perhaps it would again be the helping fixer.

2

Yendi, up-country Ghana, September 1977

Sahr and Jenny and their two daughters, Efe, 4 and Sisi, a little over a year old, arrived in Yendi to a joyous reception from the extended Akala family. A huge feast was held in their honor, with everyone in the village invited, along with members of Sahr's parents' families who came from all around. Sahr's father announced to everyone present his pride at his son's accomplishments and that, although it was a long time coming, there would finally be a modern veterinary clinic in the region that would be of great benefit to the population. He also said he was happy that his son brought such a beautiful wife and children back to his homeland, and that he looked forward to having more beautiful grandchildren in due course. He said he had been in poor health but that his spirit was rejuvenated with his son's arrival back home.

Jenny felt overwhelmed by the reception and the stares of practically everyone as she was the only white person to be seen - a tall, slim, pale skinned woman with long brown hair in a loose African linen embroidered dress that made her look taller than she was.

Although the reception was warm, it was nevertheless intimidating for her. Sahr's father, the region's biggest landowner and road and building contractor, enthusiastically introduced her personally to as many people as he could.

Sahr's mother was receptive and cordial, but nowhere near as ebullient as her husband in Jenny's presence. Sahr had explained to Jenny that his mother was a product of an ambitious family, part of the traditional political elite of the country. He told her his mother had always had an eye for protecting the family's fortunes in the ever shifting sands of Ghanaian politics. Sahr jokingly told Jenny that the country was patriarchal but that his mother was determined to make it otherwise. Jenny nevertheless looked forward to having a close relationship with her mother-in-law and believed, given time, she could achieve that. She had always managed to have good relations with just about everyone in her life. She had been looking forward to doing a Peace Corps type of community help thing, which would take shape once she got there, saw what could be done and had the family established in their new home. Perhaps her active mother-in-law could be instrumental in getting something going.

There was someone else who took an immediate interest in the lady. A young army officer in the crowd who had many dealings with the elder Akalas and Agyas observed the American woman. She is beautiful. Graceful. Elegant. Enchanting. I must have her, he thought. I don't care who she is married to. Mustafa Korafa, garrison commander, Yendi, Ghana, decided at that moment he would someday have this woman as his.

Sahr's father quickly constructed a functional building on the edge of the village to serve as the headquarters of his son's veterinary practice. There was a laboratory, a reception area, and a series of pens behind the building for segregating animals as needed, despite the fact that Sahr would be spending 90% of his time in the field amongst the herds in the countryside. It was the first true Western-style veterinary clinic in the area and Sahr quickly had a growing practice. The region was relatively well served with rainfall in the rainy season and despite long dry periods, had abundant pasture land, with many prosperous farmers and herders in the area. There was money to pay a sheep and cow doctor.

Within a few months, Jenny had developed plans for a home and school for orphaned girls in a village not far from Yendi. The town had a school that girls could go to, but parents had to pay if they wanted their female children to attend. Government support was primarily for the education of boys, to make best use of resources according to the government of the time. If parents wanted to send their daughters to school, they would have to pay the school to cover the additional cost. Some girls received some education for a few years this way, but the orphaned ones were excluded from the opportunity. Jenny spent a large amount of her time that year promoting the plan for the home and school and hostel with the in-country offices of the British and Canadian governments' aid organizations as well as that of the UN in Accra, the capital. She had made contacts with the development aid office of the US Embassy as well.

Sahr and Jenny's little girls had a difficult time at the start. There were no Saturday morning cartoons. There wasn't even any TV. No ice cream cones from Dairy Queen or weekend trips to McDonald's. But at their ages, they rapidly adjusted. They soon had a pet baby lamb their grandfather gave them. They were told they couldn't have a puppy like the one they had back in Ohio, however. Dogs were not allowed in the extended Akala family. Jenny had difficulty explaining that one to them.

There had been talk sometime after the family's arrival that the girls would have to be circumcised. Jenny knew nothing about the practice of female genital mutilation before arriving in

Africa. She was appalled when told of it. Sahr's mother had let it be known that this would have to be done. It was the way of her people. Sahr put his foot down, though. It would not be done to his daughters. He had a heated argument on the subject with his mother one day when Jenny was not around. His father arrived in the midst of the argument. Sahr later told Jenny about the encounter and said that his father had sided with him, overruling his wife and ending any discussion of it. It was never discussed again. But the incident was the spark that led Jenny to begin to question if she could have a warm relationship with her husband's mother. The distrust had begun to settle in. It was to be mutual.

Jenny's arrival in the area received a lot of attention. She was the beautiful American who became the wife of an African. No one had ever heard of that happening before in that area. People found ways to come by the Akala home, if only to look and observe how an American wife in an African home managed. One of those who showed up regularly at the Akala house was local army commander, Major Korafa, who had been at the reception after Sahr and Jenny's arrival. The garrison under his command was a small outpost, common throughout Ghana. Although not a direct relative, Korafa was a member of Sahr's mother's tribe from a neighboring region. The leaders of that tribe were influential in the area and supportive of the government that regained power the year before Sahr's return from America. The young officer visited the family to discuss politics and local affairs with Sahr and his often-present father, while being courteous and respectful of the presence of the beautiful American lady of the household. Over that time, the Major managed to refrain from letting his interest in the wife of the animal doctor of the village be known or observed in any way. There will be a time and place, he had told himself many times.

During this early period of life in Yendi, the relationship between Jenny and Sahr was much as it had been since the beginning of their years together. There continued to be an easy complicity between the two of them in the day-to-day affairs of life, an underlying passion for each other, the sharing of feelings, and a common love of their children. They could kid and tease each other like any young couple, and often did, to the occasional wonderment of members of the family who would be present.

One day in late 1979 after the family had been in Ghana for two years, Jenny received a telegram from Ohio. There was no residential telephone system in Yendi. The local post office had a telex that people used occasionally to communicate outside the country. The family back home had the telex address and used it to communicate with Jenny. The message from her sister Margie in Connecticut was very short. **Mom and Dad killed in car accident in Missouri. Sorry, Jen. Come home. Call as soon as you can.**

Jenny found a telephone she could use in the nearest town and managed to reach her sister. Their parents had been killed in an accident near St. Louis, on their way to San Diego to see their missing son's children. Jenny quickly made plans to go home and made it to Toledo for the funeral. She stayed for another three weeks to help take care of her parents' affairs, then returned to Ghana and her family.

3

February 1980

Sahr had been quiet all day. He had not said a word since sitting down for dinner. As he finished his meal, leaving half of it uneaten, he looked up and addressed his wife. "Jenny, I am taking a second wife. You will not like this, surely, but it is my prerogative." Jenny had noticed before Sahr spoke that her husband had eaten quickly, then stopped. She had barely started to eat what was on her own plate when he spoke up.

"You're what? What did you say? A second wife? What are you talking about?" replied Jenny as she stared at her husband across the table.

"I am taking a second wife. We are in Africa now. I am a Muslim. It is our way."

"What? Your way? What is this, Sahr? Your father doesn't have a second wife. What is this? What is going on?"

"I have decided to take a second wife, Jenny. The girl is from my mother's people. The decision has been made. You will have to accept it," replied Sahr. "I am sorry. But the decision is final. You will have to accept it. You are married to an African and a Muslim. Things are different here. If you do not accept it, you will have to leave."

"Leave? Sahr, what are you talking about?"

Sahr just looked at his wife and said nothing. After a moment of silence, tears swelling in her eyes, anger swelling in her thoughts, Jenny exploded: "I won't, Sahr. Do you understand? I won't."

"You will have to accept it, Jenny. It is the way here."

"This is NOT going to happen, Sahr!" Jenny was shouting. "I did not come halfway around the world with you and our daughters to be a part-time cohort! I came back here with you out of respect for you and your family. You are not going to do this to me!"

A moment of tense silence ensued, before Jenny continued "You are a real shit, Sahr. The move back here was for you. I can't believe this. What? A second wife?" Jenny's rage turned to tears. She looked at her husband. "How could you?" There was no answer.

After a few moments, Jenny rose and said to her still seated husband, "If that is the way you want it, I will take the children with me. I will go to Accra or down the road somewhere. I will not remain in a house with my husband keeping another woman."

"You will not take the children, Jenny. They will stay with me. That is also the way of Africa."

4

September 1981

Tim Hurley and Brian Maxwell had met the year before and were to work together on a project in Africa for the first time. Tim was Canadian, living and working in Montreal and Brian was an American living in Paris, where he had a management training and consulting practice. He had been hired by international aid organizations on a number of occasions over the years to provide training in Africa. When they met the year before on a consulting project in Paris, Brian had proposed to Tim that they seek challenging assignments in Africa they could work on together. Tim was interested. He had never been to Africa. He had done management training before, but had never done it in a developing country. A few months later, Tim received a call from Brian stating that he had received a contract from the United States Agency for International Development, USAID as it was called, to provide a four-day workshop for senior managers of state-run enterprises in Sierra Leone. The terms of reference stated that two trainers were to do the job. Was Tim interested in joining him? He jumped at it.

Brian and Tim would spend two days in Paris preparing the sessions before flying to Freetown, the capital of Sierra Leone. For Tim, It would be the start of a long association with Africa and the developing world.

In their discussions about the trip, Brian had suggested to Tim he go on to Ghana after the work in Sierra Leone before returning to Montreal to see if he could help an American lady he knew who was in a bit of difficulty. He related to Tim the basics of the woman's situation. With Brian's prodding, Tim booked an extension of his travel itinerary to Accra, Ghana.

Brian, his wife Alice and their two children lived in Paris in a comfy loft on the tree-lined Rue d'Alésia on the West Bank. The Maxwell apartment was the scene of many get-togethers of Americans, other expatriates and friends who found themselves in Paris for one reason or another. Tim had been a guest of Brian and Alice for an evening the previous year and was looking forward to renewing the friendship before going on to his first experience with Africa. That experience would prove to be quite an introduction to the continent and its ways.

Freetown's airport was on the opposite side of a bay. Anybody arriving by air had to take a ferry to get to the city. Cars, buses, scooters, people on foot crammed the boat, a rickety affair that Tim could see tilted slightly to one side. Just about everyone going to the city were on the bus, which was at least twenty or more years old with huge racks on the roof for whatever people were transporting - luggage, boxes of merchandise, bundles of clothing, baskets of fruits and vegetables, and other articles. Looking out the paneless windows, Tim was amused to see a half dozen chickens roaming the floor of the ferry. Women in multi-colored wrap-around robes balanced huge bundles of goods on their heads. Hundreds of people chatted away, with dust and mud everywhere. As the boat left the dock to cross the bay, Brian pointed out to Tim that the sole car on board looked to be the limousine of the North Korean ambassador to Sierra Leone. There was a little North Korean flag on the hood of the silver Mercedes, revealing the identity of the passenger inside.

At the off-loading 'ramp' on the city side which was little more than a corner of the beach, Tim and Brian watched as the ambassador's Mercedes, which was first off the ferry, became stuck in the sand. The car spinned its wheels for a good five or six minutes. The ambassador, who was dressed in a finely tailored Mao suit, emerged from the car with what looked to be his African mistress, decked out in a voluminous multi-coloured African robe. He proceeded to embark on an animated argument with her and the driver while a barking, mangy dog from the beach was trying to get a piece of his pant-leg. An amusing scene of mild chaos was unfolding. The bus couldn't get off the ferry as it was behind the Mercedes. The Ambassador, in turn, was yelling at people trying to help, telling them to get away from his pristine limousine, and kicking at the dog, which was ready to fly in the air to take a piece out of the man. Eventually, half the men on the bus descended on to the sand, pulled the ambassador aside, put multiple shoulders to the rear end of the car and it cleared the beach. Off the bus went in the dust and steamy air, meandering through the detritus of street life in this typical, bustling, boisterous African city. "My introduction to Africa," Tim laughed to his colleague.

Brian had told Tim that Sierra Leone was run by a Marxist-sympathising President-for-life, who had accepted substantial economic and military aid from China and North Korea. These included, among other things, complete turn-key infrastructure projects and sports stadiums. Many of the senior managers who were to be in the four-day training session had been trained in Beijing and Pyongyang. The two discovered, however, that some of the participants had previously worked in Europe under a free-enterprise system. What Brian and Tim talked about in the sessions was based on free-enterprise participation and reward-based management, not top-down monolithic planning, no-exceptions-allowed Communist-style obedience. It would make for interesting sessions. The clash between these two views made for some high political theatre at various times during the week. Tim and Brian were accused by a particularly strident young North-Korean trained economist of being spies for a conniving capitalist Western world intent on reversing Africa's socialist revolution. The U.S. Ambassador, a political appointee from Mississippi with deep Republican ties, did not help much on that score when he said at the opening remarks of the session, that he hoped that the session would produce a more entrepreneurial and business-focused spirit amongst the elite of Sierra Leone management. Later in the week, the Ambassador had Tim and Brian over for dinner. He spent the greater part of the evening trying to get from them what they had learned about the Communist-leaning participants in the group. He decried the fact that the recent new infrastructure in the country had been built and paid for by the Chinese and North Koreans. Tim mentioned at the dinner that he would be going on to Ghana for a few days after the sessions in Freetown. The Ambassador continued the discussion concerning Ghana by commenting on the ongoing difficulty of American companies to secure mineral development rights in that country. The Chinese were getting far more preferential treatment there. According to him, the United States needed to be more cooperative with the recently changed government to counter the Chinese influence.

Despite the ideologically-charged polemics and scepticism expressed at the start, the Canadian-American duo ended up receiving praise from virtually all of the participants at the conclusion of the session, even from the young Korean-trained economist. She said she had learned more about working with people and getting things done in the week with the two of them than she had learned in all the years of her Marxist training and education before that. The man who ran the cement company who had said the first day it was beneath him to listen to 'the dribble you are spouting' had tears in his eyes when he congratulated them on opening his mind to a more human style of management. All in all, it was a very touching end to the duo's time in Sierra Leone. Brian left the next day for Nairobi where he was to begin another assignment, while Tim flew to Accra to see Brian's American friend who needed help.

Tim's flight arrived late the following afternoon. The Canadian got off the plane and soon observed once again the general chaos of airports in Africa. Line-ups with no lines, people converging and pushing towards an entry, an exit, a control point, whatever the focus of the crowd was. People yelling, cursing, jostling, cutting in, sliding in, any manner of which to get ahead of whoever was in front. After being at what he thought to be the head of the line to claim baggage and then move on to customs, Tim soon found himself completely at the back of the line. Welcome once again to Africa, he thought.

Before leaving Paris, Brian had told Tim about his encounter on his previous trip with an American woman who worked at a travel agency in Accra. The fact that Brian had a story about someone he met did not surprise Tim. Brian Maxwell was the type of person who would strike up a friendship with just about everyone he met, regardless of circumstance. Brian related to Tim the incident of his encounter with the lady.

"She's a beautiful lady to begin with, Tim. One of the most attractive people I have ever met. Intelligent, considerate, lively at one moment, but serene and melancholic the next. I would understand why. I had no idea of how distressing her story would be. I got it all after I invited her to dinner. A truly tragic situation. Not nice. Not nice at all," Brian told Tim what he knew, encouraged him to find her in Accra and see what he could do to help. "You will be there. Maybe you can think of something. I've tried here, but with little progress. Accra is a long way from Paris."

After finally getting his luggage and clearing customs at the airport, Tim found a taxi and got himself a room in a portside hotel surrounded by a huge garden, where a monkey sat at the end of the front desk and eyed the clientele intently as they registered.

The next morning, Tim found the Africa For Sure travel agency on the main street. It was obvious which of the people there was the lady Brian had spoken about. She could not be missed – tall with long brown hair and a big smile. A striking woman, just like Brian had said, thought Tim. He introduced himself, said he was a friend of Brian Maxwell and within a few minutes he and the lady had agreed to meet for a drink at the end of the day. Tim could clearly see she was enthused about spending some time with another American, or almost-American, as she put it later.

The drink at the hotel led to an invitation for a simple dinner at Jenny's little house where they could talk more easily. She had become agitated when she learned Tim was aware of her situation. He would learn more, and in a very direct way.

5

Jay Peterson had been named chief correspondent for Africa for NewsWorld Magazine early the previous year. He had traveled far and wide since his appointment. He reported on development aid projects that had gone astray, post-colonial African politics with dictators, strongmen and attempts at democracy that never seemed to take hold. He wrote about the challenges for Americans competing with French and British interests in their former colonies, and about other political developments as they arose. As part of the mix at the time, the people of Rhodesia and Mozambique were throwing out their European masters, providing extensive content for dispatches to London. But the focus of his enquiries had lately centered on tracking the activities of China and North Korea in their buying of the favor and allegiance of regimes across the continent. Ghana was no exception. The Chinese were everywhere according to the American embassy people and expatriates he was in contact with.

"Jay, I want you to concentrate on this Chinese push for favors. Looks like Ghana is a real target now, with them doing things quite similar to what they and their Korean friends have done in Tanzania, Zambia and elsewhere. Bridges, roads to airports, stadiums. Looks familiar." Geoffrey Wilson was the senior editor of NewsWorld in London and Jay's boss and was on the line from London to Jay's room at the Accra Intercontinental.

"Precious minerals and oil are the real play here, Geoffrey," replied the correspondent. "The American companies are worried. They are not getting any meetings here with anyone. The new government is playing it cozy. Decisions on rights are not forthcoming. The process is jammed up. All sorts of Chinese around. By the way, we shouldn't talk about this on the hotel phone. The hotel is most certainly wired. Lots at stake." After a pause, Jay continued. "The current regime here is not favorable to American or British interests. Many of the people back in power were around in pre-independence days and have no love for you Brits, as you must know, nor for us Americans. I have said enough. I will find other means to reach you."

6

United States Embassy, Accra, Ghana, six months before.

Richard Keyes, forty-nine years old, veteran foreign affairs officer and a bachelor, had been the acting Chargé d'Affaires and head of consular affairs at the U.S. embassy in Accra since the previous year. It was to be his last posting. He had had enough after twenty-five years. Keyes had hoped to be made an Ambassador before bowing out. It had not happened and there was little chance it would. Word had it that the newly-elected Reagan Administration would be rewarding Republican supporters with ambassadorships, bypassing career Foreign Service officers for many of the minor postings Keyes would be eligible for. There had not been a sitting United States Ambassador to Ghana for over a year. The previous one had become ill, resigned two months after returning stateside, and had not been replaced. The elections were over. There would be a new crop of ambassadors and other political appointees.

Keyes was pretty much on his own in Accra, certainly so for consular affairs. His boss, the official Chargé d'Affaires, had been on sick leave for five months and it was not clear when he would return. In any case, the man had cared little for consular affairs, which gave Keyes the leeway to do practically what he wanted in that capacity. There were relatively few Americans in the country to begin with.

There was one confidential directive the Chargé d'Affaires had made before leaving. It was, on orders from

Washington, that the staff of the U.S. Government in Ghana was to do as little as possible to upset the government there, whoever was in charge. U.S. access to mineral rights in the country was at stake. The Chinese were at it and the U.S. had to play nice to avoid its resource companies being excluded from developing the country's vast mineral resources. There were reserves of oil as well as vast deposits of precious metals in the country. American and Chinese-owned firms were in the mix for drilling and exploration rights. Richard Keyes understood. Be nice. Don't upset the apple cart.

7

She had an aging 1972 British-made Sunbeam 4-door sedan, a little box on wheels popular with British expatriates in the former British colonies of Africa. As they wound their way over the hill from the center of town to the lane where Jenny's modest house was, she broke the silence.

"I'm upset with Brian. What I told him last year was private. I don't need to have half the world knowing my situation. It's dangerous for me. You have to realize that. You don't know half of it. I don't want to talk about it, really. Let's have some dinner and talk about other stuff. I need the company as I hope you realize, but I don't want you to think I'm inviting you to stay here tonight. It's not that..." Jenny slowed down, almost coming to a stop. "Why am I doing this?" directing the question more to herself than to the person next to her in the car. Then, to Tim, she said, "It's not fair bringing you into this. We will end up talking about it. It's my life now. I should bring you back to the hotel."

"Jenny, I'm sorry I brought this up. Bring me back, if you wish," replied Tim as they crept slowly down the poorly-lit road.

She stopped the car, looked out ahead, then turned toward her passenger. "No, I actually do need to talk. Let's have some dinner. I'll see how I feel. I'm sorry, Tim. You still on for some beans and mango salad?"

"Fine, Jenny. I'm on," replied Tim.

An hour later, after they had finished dinner with Tim conversing on and off with Buckeye, Jenny's pet parrot, who insisted on making his presence known, "He's my company these days," Jenny opened up. "It seems that Brian told you the basics of the situation I am in. There is a lot more I am not sure you know or even want to know, but I might as well give it to you. It's a mess. "

"It was a few months after my return from home and after my sisters and I buried my folks. They were killed in a car accident on the way to see my brother's kids in California. Nearly crushed me. They were my guiding lights."

"When I got back I noticed a change in my husband's attitude. Things began to be less spontaneous between us. The three weeks away seemed like they had been three months. He started giving out the authority thing, really for the first time. Things were going on in his family that I thought were behind it. His father had become seriously ill again. The cancer was back. A doctor in the provincial capital had told him he had but a few months to live. With that, his mother was showing signs of taking charge of the family. She was never really far away from that anyway in the time that I had known her. Earlier that year her cousin was made Minister of the Interior of the country, for God's sake. Got it done through the military. The army is really in charge here now; they appear to be in charge in every country in Africa for that matter. Madame's cousin was tagged to be in charge of affairs the President thought too distasteful to be involved with. With that and the influence the family had regained, the sickness of Sahr's father, the pressures of the construction business with no other son to take over, there began talk of the clan making Sahr the official chief of the tribe and also head of the family business. Sahr was not overly enthused about it. We talked about it, but it was clear he wasn't sharing everything with me."

"It kind of snowballed. He and I would have arguments we never had before. Something had changed in him. In the meantime, though, my little school for orphaned girls had received confirmation of funding from a development agency. It would be enough for a good start and two years of operations. We could apply for a continuation of the funding midway through the initial period. I was ecstatic and plowed into the preparation of the building, the recruiting of another teacher and the opening of the school a few months later. The school was important for me. Sahr knew that. My own mom was an orphan. She had spent the first seven years of her life in a dreadful orphanage in Buffalo. She told me years later when I was in my teens how three-quarters of the kids were girls and always got chosen after the boys, if at all. The school they had to go to in downtown Buffalo was horrible. I promised my Mom at the time that someday, wherever I may be, I would start an orphanage for girls that would give them, whoever they were, a chance in life." Jenny stopped, rose from the table, grabbed the pot of tea on the counter, refilled their cups, then went on.

"A couple of days after one of the Akala family meetings, meetings that I was not allowed to attend, Sahr dropped the bomb. He told me he was taking another wife. Said it was the African way."

"Just like that. He said he hoped I could accept it, while implying that I had no choice. Another wife?! I couldn't believe what he was saying. I lost it. Went ballistic. There was no way I was going to accept another woman in our home, accept that I would be sharing my husband with someone else? No way. I told him he was not going to do it. I didn't care if it was the African way. It was not part of our deal. We did not have a Muslim marriage. We had been married in a Catholic church. He had taken a vow, just as I had. He said he didn't care about that. We were in Africa now and the rules were different. He said that if I left the home he would be keeping the girls with him. I stalked out of the room where we were and left him there. I didn't really believe him on the bit about keeping the girls. He did not come to the bedroom. We never shared a bed from that night forward."

Jenny took a sip from her cup, then continued. "The next morning he told me he was serious and that I would have to accept his decision. I said I would not, and that regardless of what he had said about keeping the children if I left, that was not going to happen. We had an incredible row, just like the one the night before. He ended up saying I would have to leave - then, and without the girls. He was throwing me out. I couldn't believe it, Tim. He said he was not going to change his mind about the second wife and that, whatever I had to say, the children would be staying with him. That is the African way as well, he said."

Jenny had trouble containing her tears as she spoke, but continued. "He wouldn't even let me say goodbye to my girls. His mother had taken them to the other side of the village. He gave me 30 minutes to put my clothes together and pack. As I remember it, all I could say to him as I walked out was, "You shit, Sahr! All we have gone through. And taking the girls away from me! You shit! He just looked at me. Said nothing."

"I came here. I had money in a bank back in Ohio. Dad had done well in life. I didn't need Sahr's money, thank God. I needed a job to occupy my time, though, while I worked to get custody of the girls. I would go nuts if I didn't have something to do. I couldn't leave the country. I was scared I would not be able to get back in. I would need a re-entry visa. The key minister of the country was and still is a member of Sahr's family. He could block everything. It would be very easy. I could be cut off for good from my children."

"Have you had any contact with your kids? Anything at all?"

"Nothing gets to the girls, apparently. Word is that I abandoned them. A wanton American slut, that is what people are being told. That's what the lady who helped me with the orphanage said the last time I spoke with her. She asked me not to send her any more letters. There is telephone service now in Yendi. I call and, except for one or two people who accept to talk to me, they hang up. But, I can't leave here. If I do, I'm sure I'll never get back in."

Jenny sighed, looked at Tim across the table and continued. "I tried twice to get the girls and leave the country. A couple months after coming here, I found someone to go to Yendi to take the girls and bring them back here. We would then hook up and go to the Embassy to take refuge. American children being held away from their American mother. Question of protecting American citizens. I would take my chances on getting the Embassy to get us out and back to the States. That was before I understood that the Embassy was probably not going to help. I will explain that. In any case, the man I hired was recommended to me by a friend who I met here and was sympathetic to my situation. The guy was a former policeman. Retired. Said he knew the area. I gave him the equivalent of a thousand dollars up front with another two thousand to be paid upon his return with the children. Gave him the upfront money and then never saw him again. He just took the money and ran. Through it all, the police somehow learned what I tried to do and I received a warning. Soon after, one of the nemeses of my life now showed up in person - Colonel Korafa, the local garrison commander who had been so nice in Yendi and is now head of the country's intelligence service."

"Anyhow, the first attempt to get the girls was a fiasco. You can't trust many people around here. You have to pay people to get things done, anything done, and even then, you are never sure you are going to get what you have paid for. So I decided to do it myself. I decided to go up there, grab the girls and make a run to the border, cross it in the middle of the bush at night, go to Ouagadougou, then on to Paris and the States. I bought an old Land Rover which was still in good shape, the best map I could find and a compass, hired a young man to come with me for protection and set out for Yendi. I would grab the girls in the middle of the night when everyone was asleep, say Mommy was back and that we were going to go back to Ohio and their cousins and friends. They could have Dairy Queen again. Daddy would join us later. Well, I got about fifty kilometers up the highway when an army vehicle forced us off the road. Soldiers came out with guns pointed, told us to get in the back seat and drove us back to Accra. When we got back, Korafa was waiting. Basically wants me to sleep with him. Obsessed with me. Makes no bones about it. Never saw the Land Rover again. I went to recover it a few days later and was told it got wrecked. Sorry, they said. I only have the Sunbeam now."

Jenny was set to continue, but Tim interrupted. "What about the Embassy here? The U.S. Government? They couldn't help? Your kids are American citizens. They are being sequestered and their American mother prevented from having access to them. Seems like something they should take on."

"That's something else in all of this. My government has done nothing for me. The consular affairs guy here is a real s.o.b.

Says he wants to help, but he does nothing. He's actually after me to have an affair with him. Pursues me. Obsessive. Has asked me to dinner ten times if not twice. The travel agency is just up the street from the embassy's consular office. He comes to the agency regularly. All sorts of excuses to come by. He will invariably come over and quietly ask me to dinner or for a drink. Says he needs to talk to me. I went once and it was clear he wanted me to sleep with him. Blatant. No disguising it. Four months ago, I went to the embassy, spoke to someone I knew about the consular head not appearing to do anything about my children. I refrained from saying anything about the harassment. That visit ended up putting the person I spoke to in a delicate position. The guy doing this, Keyes, is the person in charge there these days. No Ambassador, no number two. I got nowhere. Keyes found out I had spoken to my contact there about his activities, or lack thereof. Said I misunderstood and that I should not complain anymore. He would certainly not help me with my kids if I spoke to anyone again at the embassy. Basically, what he implies through all of this is 'Sleep with me, Jenny, and then maybe I can help you'. A disgusting man."

Jenny paused, took a deep breath, then looked up at the ceiling before continuing. "I was 20. A flower child. Did not think through any of this. Romantic. Such a beautiful idea. But I had no idea, really. I was infatuated. It was a physical thing as well. An elegant, gentle African Zeus who I brought to bed rather than the other way around. So different from the guys who would date me in those years. Frat boys and the like out for lots of beer and good lays before they went off to Vietnam or a job in a big company. But I didn't look very far out about this. I certainly had no idea of what went on in Africa...... I have two beautiful daughters that have been cut off from me. How could I have foreseen this?"

It was after 9 o'clock by that time and dark outside.

At that moment, a huge bright light blazed through the large window at the front. The light went off, then came back on. The glaring high-beam light illuminated the far wall. On and off. Five times. Buckeye cried out, "Lights. Lights." Then silence.

"It's a warning to you, Tim. You will have to leave."

"What do you mean, a warning? From who?"

"The colonel. The guy I told you about before we got on to the Embassy. Colonel Korafa. He is a member of my mother-in-law's tribe, a second or third cousin or something. His connection to the family was never made fully clear to me. In any case, he knows everything I do. I'm certain he has my phone at the office tapped. He knew all about the Land Rover trip to Yendi, had his men intercept me. He wants me to become his mistress. Says he will protect me. Now that I have been thrown out of the house by my husband, I am apparently fair game. Local rules. He doesn't want anybody else around. He has the run of Accra. I have to put up with this, Tim. In the meantime, the flashing lights are for you. Those are his guys out there."

"You mean to tell me that you are being harassed by both the chief representative of the U.S. Government in this country as well as the head of the local Gestapo?"

"I wouldn't put it quite that way, but yes, I am being pursued by these people. I can't change it. I just have to resist as long as I can. If I leave here, it's all over. I'll never get back in. I'm sure of it. That's what my husband's family wants. I can't believe he does too, but it looks that way. You must leave now, Tim. He's warning you. I will call a taxi."

"No, no, Jenny. I am not going to leave you this way. Forget the taxi."

"What else are you going to do? Stay here until he shows up with a couple of his goons, takes you outside and beats you up, then leaves you on the side of the road somewhere? Believe me, they do that here. Canadian, American, whatever. They will deny everything, then insist on you leaving the country. Don't try to be a hero. It won't help me at all."

Tim left Jenny's little house, crossed the scrubby dirt yard to the road where the taxi waited in silence in the hot night air. A black four-wheel drive was parked further down the road with the moonlight reflecting off its hood. Like a panther waiting to strike in the night, thought Tim. There was no other vehicle in sight. Scared. She has every reason to be. Not many friends for her in this place. Dangerous for anyone who would be. The family for her is gone. Alone. Pursued. Stalked. He got into the taxi and told the driver where to take him.

Tim tried to reach Jenny the following day. He went to the agency. No Jenny. Receptionist said she had taken the day off. Could he have her telephone number at her house? No, he couldn't, said the receptionist. He left a message for Jenny to call him when she could, leaving the number at the hotel. Before taking a taxi back to the hotel, he walked up the street and found a table at the outdoor cafe across the road from the Embassy. Need to see who this consul guy could be, Tim thought. He had been sitting there for not more than a minute when he noticed a black Toyota Land Cruiser slowly coming to a stop across the street. Was it the same one in the street the night before? He couldn't tell. He could see that two men were in the vehicle. Nobody got out. The same vehicle was outside the entrance to the hotel grounds that morning as he left. It was clear. He was being watched. Serious stuff going on here, he thought. What can I do for this lady? He remained at the cafe for close to two hours. The Land Cruiser did not budge and no middle-aged American male entered or left the embassy consular section office across the street during that time. This is dumb. Back to the hotel.

He went down to the dining room at seven to have some dinner and observed a young couple at one of the tables. They looked to be Americans. The waiter brought him to a table not far from theirs. Tim had just finished his meal when the young man leaned around and asked Tim if he wanted to join them. "Hello, you look to be American. We have noticed you sitting there alone. Would you like to join us for coffee and dessert?"

Tim smiled. "Not American. Canadian. Sorry. But, come to think of it, I would be glad to join you if I don't have to be an American."

"Certainly not required," laughed the man. "Come on over."

"Hello, my name is Jay Peterson. This is my friend Amy Leach who works with me. We're journalists. We work for NewsWorld magazine. Amy covers French West Africa and the Maghreb countries while I cover the rest of this enchanting continent. We happen to be here at the same time by chance. Amy's on the way back to Dakar and I'm here for a few days. We were at the Intercontinental but decided to come here for the balance of our stay. A bit more rustic and we like the monkey. And you?"

"Jay, Amy. Pleased to meet you. My name is Tim Hurley. I'm from Montreal. I work in consulting. I'm here on a private trip after finishing an assignment over in Sierra Leone. Thanks for inviting me over. Good to talk to some people from the world we know, n'est ce pas?"

"Yes, n'est ce pas. Things are different here, that's for sure."

The three expats, alone by that time in the hotel dining room, spent the next hour talking about what they do, about Africa, about people and places, then broke up for the rest of the evening and found their rooms.

8

Tim couldn't sleep. He got up, went to the window overlooking the bay, and it came to him. The next morning, he went to the dining room to be there when it opened. Around 7:30, Jay Peterson walked in and quickly observed Tim motioning to him to join him at his table.

"What another beautiful morning on the Gold Coast," said Jay as he sat down. "The monkey at the front desk is too much. Watches everybody and observes intently everything they do. How are you, Tim? I enjoyed our discussion last night."

"Where is Amy? She not coming down to breakfast?"

Jay replied. "No. She's out of here. Had an early flight to Dakar. We said our goodbyes in the hallway last night. She's a good correspondent and a good buddy. We started at NewsWorld the same day four years ago."

Jay looked across the table. "You look preoccupied about something. What's up? Have I said something?"

"No, Jay. Sorry. I do have something to share with you, though. I have been pondering whether I should tell you about it since last evening."

"Well, what is it? Something I can help you with?"

"It's about a lady. Here, in Ghana. An American. She's in a bind. A big one. U.S. Government should be helping her but is not. I have been made aware of her situation, but am at a loss as to what I can do. I'll tell you her story, if you want to hear it, and you can decide if you want to dig into it."

"Tell me. I'm a correspondent. It is why you are telling me this. I know that, and it's all right, but tell me. An American lady in a bind in an African country and the US government doesn't want to help her. Let's hear it."

Tim proceeded to tell him everything he knew of Jenny's situation.

Jay quickly understood that what he had just heard could be a blockbuster. "Tim, this could be big. Lots of newsworthy stuff. An American running into African culture, a mother losing access to her kids because of it. Intelligence chief blackmailing American lady, possible sexual harassment here by a U.S. government official as part of all this." Jay had in mind the possibility of the U.S. government sacrificing the interests of a citizen to protect U.S. company interests in this country - the mining rights stuff and everything around it - but he held back on mentioning it to Tim. "Heavy stuff. Need to know more. Will the lady speak to me?"

"Let me try. I don't know of any other way to help her. Give me a couple of hours. You'll be here?" said Tim.

"I'm around. Won't be far. My flight out of here is two days from now."

Tim Hurley postponed his flight to Paris so he could stay another day. He went again to the travel agency. Jenny was not there. Nobody would or could say when she would be in. The Canadian parked himself across the street in the outside bar under an awning and waited for Jenny to hopefully show up sometime that day.

A little after 11, Jenny entered the agency. Tim rose, crossed the street and went in. He noticed the same black Land Cruiser was parked halfway down the block.

"Jenny, I need to speak with you."

"Tim, what are you doing here? I thought you had left. You can't be here. The colonel's people are right down the street."

"I know, I saw them. Jenny, listen to me. There may be a way to get some action from people to help you. I want you to meet someone. He is the chief correspondent for this part of Africa for NewsWorld magazine. I told him your story. He wants to meet you. Hear it from you."

"You what? You told him my story? Tim, do you realize what you are doing? You could be making it worse for me."

"Jenny, listen. You don't have many other options. You told me so yourself. A story in NewsWorld would shake the U.S. Government into defending you. It would embarrass the government here to no end. They can't afford to look to be so mean to foreigners. They need expatriates here. It could shake the tree. I think it is worth it, Jenny. What else will you do?"

Jenny took a moment, looking at Tim, before replying. "OK then. But I won't meet with him. He already has the story. You told him everything, right? If I meet with him, the colonel's boys will see it. He wants to talk to me. We can do it by telephone instead, but not from here."

Who is this guy messing around? Canadian. Here on a visit. Got a visitor's visa from the embassy in Freetown. The colonel in charge of intelligence for the Government of Ghana knew everything about the comings and goings of the American woman. The last contact with her had been three weeks before. She rebuffed him. She always does. Been this way for a year, thought the officer as he contemplated the short report from his lieutenant. She will change her mind eventually. The kids. All about the kids. She won't leave this place. And the consul. What an idiot. A nuisance. I could get him into real trouble with his government. In the meantime, the man serves my purpose. But this Canadian. At her place the other night. My guys scared him off. But.....speaking with the guy from the magazine at the hotel. Twice. What's he up to?

Jay Peterson succeeded in reaching Jenny later that day. The lady had balked at speaking with him, but he finally reached her at the cafe. She had given Tim the number.

"Mrs. Akala, this is Jay Peterson. I understand that Tim Hurley has told you of our discussion."

"You don't have to call me Mrs. Akala. I would prefer Jenny. Yes, Tim told me he had spoken with you. I must be careful. I hope you understand that."

"Of course. Jenny. I understand. Could we meet? I may have a way to help you. A telephone discussion would probably be the least secure way to talk about anything involved with this, however. I am calling from the American Express office but the call could nevertheless be traced. People listen in to what just about anyone of any consequence in this town has to say. Do you have a quiet place where we could meet? If we don't meet, I'm afraid I can't go very far with this. Are you on?"

"OK. I'm on. I can meet you at the restaurant The Sand Dune on the Accra - Cape Coast Road west of the city at seven tomorrow evening. Is that all right?" Before Jay could respond, she continued, "You are sure of this, Mr. Peterson? Nobody will know about our meeting?"

"Nobody. Seven is fine. See you then."

The agent of state security took off his headphones and headed to the office of the colonel.

So she is going to meet a newsman. American, I gather, with a big magazine. What is he doing in all of this? She is complicating matters. I don't like this, said the intelligence chief to himself as the agent left the room.

Jay Peterson decided to extend his stay in Accra. After the call with the lady, he received a message from Geoffrey to call him. He called using the phone at the American Express office.

"Jay, I want you to follow up on something. The desk in Chicago called me and told me they had received a tip about a company called Hedman Resources of Cleveland. The company had apparently paid a huge sum to a Ghanaian government insider - we understand it to be the Minister of the Interior - to secure rights to a bevy of choice deposits of precious metals in the country. It's stuff that goes into micro-chips and aerospace components and the like. Strategically important material. It was a big payoff, apparently. Some people in Washington know about it, but it is not something they want known, even by their own diplomats or staff in Accra. Would not be good for the government to have the American public aware that US companies were paying government ministers in Africa. And that their government knew all about it. We spoke about the

Chinese connection the other day. This is part of it. Americans paying to beat the Chinese. New government there is apparently playing ball. Washington wants to keep a lid on the whole thing. Go to it. Find out what you can. Stay away from the Embassy, though."

Minister of the Interior..Minister of the Interior..Didn't Tim tell me the lady's mother-in-law's cousin was the Minister of the Interior? This is getting interesting.

9

"So, who's the Canadian, Jenny?" The consul had approached her from behind. Jenny had chanced going to the restaurant with Margaret Bishop of the aid organization that had facilitated the grant for the school two years before. She was hoping they would not be seen by one of her antagonists. The lunch had been scheduled for some time and she didn't want to put it off. Margaret was busy and not often in Accra for get-togethers. She had gone to the rest room and Richard Keyes took advantage of the moment.

"You've been watching me, Keyes. Leave me alone. You have done nothing to help me. It's clear you have no intention of doing so. So, just stay out of my life."

Richard Keyes had a spy at the restaurant where Jenny and the Canadian had had a drink together three evenings before. He paid the waiter a small sum to report whenever he saw the lady in the restaurant and describe what he observed. He had received the report of the encounter with the man new to Accra along with a photograph. He matched the photo with the face of the guy he saw through the window of the Embassy spending so much time across the street the day before. Keyes thought he was watching the building, hoping to see someone in particular either entering or leaving. Who was he trying to identify? Me? What did Jenny tell him?

"Madame Akala, what you are requesting is delicate and difficult to accomplish," said Keyes. "You are asking the United

States Government to have the Government of Ghana make an exception to their laws on family and marriage. They can just say "No, Mr. Keyes, we cannot do what you ask," and that would be it. Further, your husband's family members are in charge of much of what happens in this country. This is a difficult thing to accomplish. The timing and circumstance of the request and any other contacts in this regard have to be just right. I am trying the best I can to find the right circumstance. I am sorry." What he did not say was that things were more complicated than that. Jenny's mother-in-law's cousin controlled the awarding of mineral rights in Ghana and that was a problem. Richard Keyes was not going to do anything that would upset the man. Intervening on Jennifer Sutton Akala's behalf would certainly do that.

"Keyes, you are doing nothing about this. And I am sure you will not unless I agree to sleep with you. Now leave me alone." At that moment, Margaret returned to the table and wondered what had been going on. The consul turned and made for the door.

"Who was that, Jenny? You look distressed."

"Somebody I can't stand. Let's order our lunch." Jenny was not quite ready to tell other people in Accra of the depth of the difficulties she was having with nasty men in Ghana. She had already told Margaret months ago about the difficulties with her husband's family and the need to suspend the development of the school. Funds had not been disbursed to Jenny's school as yet, in any case. The organization considered the project to be on hold. Schools for girls usually encountered problems in Africa.

Have to watch the Canadian. Is he still around? Did Jenny tell him anything? Could this be trouble? Richard Keyes walked back to the Embassy.

The following day, 6:45 AM

Jay Peterson observed the envelope on the floor in front of the door of his room. Somebody had slipped it under the door. Probably the bill, he thought as he picked it up. It was not a bill. It was simply a sheet of paper with a typed note on it - **Stay out of affairs here. Better if you leave things alone.** The note was signed **'a friend.'**

The sun was down. Jay's taxi had been on the road for close to an hour, trying to find the restaurant. Here it is. It IS out of the way. He found her at a table in a secluded corner. Tim was right. She is striking. "Hello. You are Jenny, I presume?"

"Yes, that is me. Welcome to out of the way suburban Accra, Mr. Peterson. Please sit down," replied the woman.

Their eyes met. Sadness and fear, he thought. "I understand you are in a predicament. How else can I put it?"

"I guess you could put it that way." Jenny hesitated, looking back, wondering if she could trust the person in front of her. What do I tell him? All of it? Part of it? thought Jenny. After a moment, she simply asked the question, "Do you think you can help me?"

"You need to tell me a few things. For sure. But, yes, I think I can, if only based on what I have been told."

She decided to unload. "Where do I need to start?"

"Why not from the beginning. I'll order a beer in the meantime."

During her 'unload' as she called it, that took up the better part of two hours, they managed to finish a dinner of lamb and rice, with Jenny continually keeping an eye on the door. She was never sure no one was following her or observing what she was doing, no matter where she was. It was her ongoing nightmare. Jay took it all in. This is real. No making this stuff up, he thought. Entirely believable.

"Do you want this to be public, Jenny? Tell me. I can make it look bad for the U.S. government and for the government here. Would not be nice for its image in the world. If I write something, which I am inclined to want to do and it gets published, the U.S. government will most likely be shamed into doing something, but will it get your children back? It may not work. The government here just may say no. You would probably have little choice but to leave. But, I guess the alternative is to continue living in your hell with consequences for your daily life which could be worse. But you have to tell me. Do we do this?"

"We do it. I can't go on this way."

Jay left the restaurant and got into the taxi. The black limousine followed. On a dark unlighted stretch of the road, the limousine pulled up alongside with the passenger in the front seat motioning to the driver of the taxi to pull over. The Mercedes came to a stop in front at an angle preventing the taxi from advancing. A man in dark sunglasses emerged, walked slowly over, ordered the passenger out of the car, motioned him to the far side out of earshot of the driver, and then addressed him, with his face close to Jay's. Barely a foot separated the two men from each other. "No more meeting or speaking to the American lady. Understood?" It was given in almost a whisper, but with menace.

"Hmm.. I won't ask who you are, but message received. I'll give it consideration," replied the correspondent, wondering how far he could go. He has a gun. Can't be too brave here.

"No, you won't just give it consideration. This is serious. Stay away. Am I understood, sir?" replied the man in a deep voice. "And, no writing about this. Do you understand me?"

Before the journalist could respond, Colonel Mustafa Korafa turned, went to the driver side of the taxi, said something to the driver, then got into the back seat of the limousine and drove away.

Jay got back into the taxi and could see the driver's hands shaking as the old man managed to grip the wheel before regaining the road. I think I just had an encounter with the colonel, thought the correspondent.

The colonel called Jenny the next day at work. "What are you doing, Jenny? What are you telling a newsmagazine correspondent over a two-hour dinner? What have you discussed with Mr. Peterson?"

With a mix of fear and anger, Jenny replied, "A fellow American, Major Korafa. It's none of your business."

"It's Colonel now, Jenny. So childish a slight. I can decide what to do with you here. You know that. Be careful. Very careful."

10

Three days later, Jenny's boss, a Brit who had bought the agency a few years before, called her into his office.

"Jenny, I have to terminate your engagement. Seems you have been consorting with customers, and the government objects to that on the part of people who welcome foreigners to the country here. Against the rules, in any case. You know it, even if it is bogus. We have spoken about it before. I got a call yesterday from a government official who has seen you in restaurants with visitors in animated discussions and then leaving with the men at the end of the meal late at night. Pictures here - one with a Canadian a few days ago, one with an American a few months ago, and the latest one with another American in another restaurant earlier this week. The government official who called said your actions do not sit well for the agency to receive a continuation of its permit. Says he thinks you are prostituting."

"What? Prostituting? Incredulous, John. What is this?"

"I know. Believe me, I know it, Jenny. But if I continue to employ you, I will not receive an extension of my license to operate a ticketing agency. It is ludicrous. I know none of it is true. But the bottom line is I can't continue to have you work here. I know your situation with your children. I don't know what else to say. I have little leeway in the matter. They have made it clear. I'm sorry."

Jenny could not believe what she was hearing. She was getting fired. No more job. Korafa. The son of a bitch. Jenny looked at her boss, rose without saying a word, and walked out the door.

Korafa showed up at the house the next evening. He knocked on the door. Jenny opened it and immediately yelled at the man on the doorstep. "You bastard, Korafa! You had me fired. You are a rat. Keep away from me," and tried to shut the door.

Korafa blocked the door and entered, grabbed Jenny by the arm and threw her onto the large-cushioned sofa. He wasted no time. He ripped open her blouse and drew her skirt off her hips while she pounded on his chest to ward off the attack. In the scuffle, Jenny managed to grab Korafa's pistol protruding from his hip holster, drew it out and put the barrel to his head.

"Get out, you monster. Now. I know how to use this. I mean it. You will not rape me, you menacing, despicable animal," said Jenny to the man.

Korafa rose, straightened his tunic, walked to the door, then turned. "I will expect you to be out of the country by the end of the week. I am sorry it could not have been a nicer relationship. Please leave the gun on the table when you leave. Goodbye, Jenny."

I went too far, he thought as he opened the door of his car. He had come alone. He sat behind the wheel a moment before turning the key. Adventure over. She will be out of here soon. Just as well.

Jenny placed the call to the clinic in Yendi. Sahr answered.

Without even a hello, she yelled her anger at her husband. Sahr always had someone else answer the phone and had not returned a call from Jenny since she had left eighteen months before. She was surprised she got him. Just as well, she thought. "Sahr, you listen to me! I was nearly raped by Korafa last night! Raped! Are you happy with what you have done to me?!"

"What? Korafa? Rape you?"

"Yes. Rape - by the supposed friend of the great Akala family! He ripped my clothes half off. I am fair game, I guess. This is what you have wrought on me. I saved myself from the indignity by grabbing his gun and turning it on him. I didn't have to use it, but it is what saved me from him."

Jenny angrily continued, "This is what you have brought on me. The mother of your children, the lady you supposedly loved and brought to Africa, to your people! What you have done to me. For what? Another wife, a teenager. How disgusting, Sahr. Such a betrayal. All we lived together. All we shared."

Tears were streaming down Jenny's face as she finished what she had to say. "The man I knew and loved is gone. And I will be soon. I can't continue this. You have won, Sahr. I can't go on here. I have never understood that you could actually do it with no regret, no remorse. Still can't believe it. But it's not over. The children will hate you some day and will come to me. By whatever means, I will be re-united with them. That day will come."

"Jenny, wait. The rape thing. It was not supposed to come to this. You would have continued to be my preferred wife. The second one was for political reasons. I had to do it."

"Well, it has come to this. And 'the had to do it' stuff. Please, spare me that. You could have said no. It would not have changed anything. You're a shit, Sahr. A real shit. Goodbye."

Jenny then placed a call to the hotel. She caught Jay Peterson just as he was preparing to make a visit to the Embassy.

"Jay, I'm leaving. I've had it. You can do what you want. Korafa tried to rape me last night. He got me fired from my job. They have won. I'm out of here. Can't take it any longer. Have to find another way for my kids. Goodbye." With that, Jenny hung up before Jay had a chance to say anything. He tried to reach her, but the agency said she no longer worked there and had no forwarding address, nor telephone number. There was no answer at her house. Where was she going?

A little after two in the morning, two men entered the hotel through an unlocked back entrance, climbed the stairs to the third floor, picked the lock of Jay's room, entered, put a hood over the reporter's head as he stirred from his sleep and administered a number of punches before telling him "Get out of here. No stories from Accra. Last warning," then left.

That does it, a dazed Jay Peterson, reporter, told himself. Now I will write it up. The son-of-a-bitch. The lady will be out of here by the time it gets anywhere.

The colonel received the call at his office four days later. It was from the office of the military chief of staff. He was to come to the COS' office the next day.

"What is this about?" Korafa asked.

"You will find out. Just be here at 9 o'clock tomorrow."

Korafa arrived expecting to be received by the chief of staff of the Ghanaian army who was the de facto strongman of the government and someone Korafa knew well. The man had put Korafa in charge of military intelligence two years before. Instead, he was ushered into a small room where he was met by an army staff colonel accompanied by two soldiers. "Colonel Korafa, your duties will be changing. You will be the new warden of the military prison up north, starting next Monday. You know the prison well, I understand. You have been relieved of your command of the intelligence service. I must ask you for the keys to your office as well as the keys to your vehicle. Lieutenant Okese from my staff will be driving you to your office and then to your quarters. I wish you well in your new duties."

Korafa was stunned. "Wait a minute. What is this about? I am being demoted?... For what reason? What have I done? Our government is secure...our borders are secure....our enemies here are under control....the President is safe. What is this about?"

"You did it to yourself, Colonel. Couldn't keep your hands off of a lady.....wife of a member of the Interior Minister's family, no less. Bad indiscretion....very bad.....not wise. You tried to rape her, Korafa. You are lucky to not be put in that jail you are going to."

"She is a slut. Her husband disowned her. Threw her out. She's nothing," replied Korafa. The officer looked at him with a hint of disdain, then turned and left, leaving the two soldiers to escort a stunned Colonel Mustafa Korafa out the door.

The bitch. I am being humiliated and ruined. Prison in the north. Exile. She got to her husband before she left. I knew I went too far.... I guess Akala, the doctor of cows and goats, has some feelings for her after all.... I'll get back at all of them. The future is a long time. In the meantime, I will mark my time, make the best of the situation. I know a lot about what is going on here. People are going to pay. Colonel Korafa who was now Major Korafa once again and warden of the desolate Dibele military prison of the Government of Ghana for dissidents and opponents of the regime, worked his way through his desk and his personal effects, then asked the escorting Lieutenant to arrange for his transport to the prison the next morning. "Let's get on with it."

Jenny left Accra within 48 hours of her encounter with Korafa. After the telephone call with her husband, she called her landlord to tell him she would be vacating the house. She had reached the British Airways ticket office at the airport and booked her own flight to London and on to New York. She sold her Sunbeam for a decent price to a waiter at the restaurant down the street from the agency. She called Margaret Bishop - told her she was leaving and that whatever funds for the school project that were being held should be released and affected to other projects. There would be no school for orphaned girls in Yendi, at least not one that she would be directing. She accepted Margaret's offer to take Buckeye. He would continue to have a loving friend. She did not let the Embassy know she was leaving. She would spare the consul the news. He would have to find some other woman to pursue. She just left, but not before sending another letter to her girls. Number seventeen she figured, and with probably no response, just like all the others.

In late afternoon the day that Jenny Akala left Ghana, Jay Peterson sat down at the desk in his hotel room, brought out his portable typewriter and typed at the top of the page 'The Lady from Toledo.........'

PART TWO

11

Jay Peterson had a degree in journalism from the University of Missouri and had begun his career with the Kansas City Star. After two years there he had moved on, getting a job as investigative reporter for the Los Angeles Times. Before long, Jay became known for uncovering corruption in the Los Angeles Police Department. His articles were certain to get him into trouble and they did. Elements in the LAPD did not appreciate what he was writing. He received a number of anonymous threats. At about the same time, his wife, who had been with him since his second year in college, left him for a jazz musician she had met in San Francisco. He didn't see it coming. He didn't think he had neglected his wife and best friend, but he had - the lifestyle and preoccupations of her investigative reporter husband had soured the relationship. By 1977, Jay had decided to leave Los Angeles. Through a friend in New York, he received word that NewsWorld Magazine was looking for a correspondent who was equally conversant in French and English and could work in Europe. Jay fit the bill. He had grown up in Chicago, son of a Sears Roebuck executive who had met a French lady when stationed in Europe and married her. Jay spoke both French and English from an early age. He had never lost it. Throughout their lives, he and his two younger brothers spoke to their mother and she to them in French, although she had lived in the United States for close to thirty years.

The job with NewsWorld involved having a base in Paris while covering European political affairs. Within a year, there emerged a need for a head person for Africa and he was tapped for it. He would be based in Abidjan and report to a managing director in London. Jay Peterson had not had a love in his life since his time in L.A. A female friend or two in Paris, but nothing serious. As he wrote the first lines of The Lady from Toledo, he thought that in another time and place, he could fall for her. Won't happen. Too complicated. He spent the next four hours writing the story of the American lady caught up in the customs and intrigues of Africa.

Over the weeks following the submission of the story, Jay could not get an answer from his boss. "When will the story appear? Will it appear?"

"Coming, Jay. We're looking at it. Stay cool," were Geoffrey's words on the subject in the three times they had spoken about it.

Jay got the call from Geoffrey as he was leaving the office one day for a flight to Nairobi. "We're not doing it, Jay."

"We're not doing what, Geoffrey? The story on the lady?"

"The story on the lady. Too much is up in the air about it. Only one source. Nobody else. You did not manage to get any corroborating evidence from anybody else, Jay. Words of a Canadian consultant who was in Accra for three days about a mysterious lady you hardly spent any time with. Nobody else down there knows anything about it. It's why we have taken all this time. We called the Embassy. A person we finally reached after multiple tries knew nothing of a Jenny Sutton Akala, who was supposed to have had all these contacts with consular officials. Giving a fake reason for our call, we asked her to check with colleagues and we would call back. We did. The lady said the same thing. Nobody knew anything of a Jennifer or Jenny

Sutton Akala. We asked a chap we know in Accra, an old hand from colonial days, to check out a Colonel Korafa, head of intelligence. According to our man, nobody knew of a Colonel Korafa. According to the Government of Ghana, the man doesn't exist. Jay, I don't doubt your seriousness in this, but there is just no way we can go with a story with such slim bonafides. Sorry. Drop it. Move on."

"What? Geoffrey, I don't believe this. I was threatened, beaten up about this. What more does it take? This is real. She is real. Her situation is real. We have collusion on the part of the U.S. Government, collusion to ignore the plight of an American citizen and American-born children. This is all real, Geoffrey. Special deal for American resource company. Don't rock the boat. Sacrifice an American mother in the process. Not right, Geoffrey."

"Sorry, Jay. We're not doing it. Move on. Can we talk about something else?"

"Geoffrey, we can talk about something else, but I am not happy about this. I got beat up. My life was threatened. The Canadian guy was threatened as well. We didn't make this shit up." Jay Peterson paused a moment, then said in mild anger, "What do you want to talk about?"

12

It had taken two days to pack up. She left whatever possessions she was not taking with her to the family that lived down the lane. A bit of furniture, some clothes, dishes and pots and pans. Whatever the family wanted they could have. They took everything that was offered. Whatever they could not use, they could sell. Somebody would pay something for just about anything in Accra.

She went through the motions of shutting things down with a mixture of grief, of anger, then melancholy, then back to anger with the cycle continuing to work through her. She was leaving her children, which she never thought she would do. Tears came. The despair would consume her for long moments ....Then the flight, the arrival in Toledo, the days afterward. Part of the emptiness she felt would always be there. She knew that. It would be a difficult time. She wondered daily if she had made the right decision. She could have stayed. Maybe things would have changed. The doubt consumed her.

Her sister Margie insisted that Jenny stay with she and her family for awhile. There was nothing anymore in Toledo. That part of her life was gone. No Mom and Dad anymore, friends dispersed, her sisters living elsewhere. After three nights at a hotel, visits to the cemetery and nowhere else to go, she called Margie and told her she would be coming to Connecticut.

The depths of her depression lasted six months. What had started in her last days in Accra only got worse. She couldn't sleep. She spent days in her room, losing track of time, pacing the floor.

One morning she announced to Margie and her husband Bob that she was the incarnation of the devil. She had caused the perversion of her daughters, she was the temptress that caused men to sin, it was all her fault. She knew all about hell. She had felt the fire during the night. Margie found a psychiatrist and convinced Jenny she needed to see him. Jenny went to see the man, an elderly Serb, a refugee from communist Yugoslavia. Before leaving the old country, he had seen over and over the despair of mothers who had lost their children in war and its aftermath, who had been subjected to rape, had lost their self-respect, had been to Jenny's depths and beyond. The old Serb would be a god-send for her. They met regularly. He put her on an anti-depressant and she began to sleep again, She came to realize her situation was not of her doing. She would come out of the depression like an energetic lioness, roaring, determined and ready to take on the world, in the words of the psychiatrist at their last meeting. But a part of her was gone. The bubbly and engaging Jenny Sutton that everyone knew had become more private, introspective and less trusting of others.

At the end of those months of depression, she woke up one day and decided that the inactivity had to end. Her life had to move on. She would continue to write to her children, would pressure her government to do something, go to the UN. But she needed something to do. She called Doug, her former boss at the ad agency in Columbus where she had worked eight years before. She told him the basics of her situation and that she needed a job. Did he know anyone in New York who could use someone like her? Doug Brady did not hesitate. "Jenny, let me work on it. I will be glad to help you. Sure you don't want to come back to Columbus? You could work here."

"No, Doug, I need to be near the UN and our government in DC. Need to work those people to get my daughters back. It may be fruitless. I may be dreaming about the UN stuff and all but I have to try. Hopefully, I can find something in New York. I hope you understand."

"Got it. Understand. Let me work on it."

A week later she had an interview at McGuire Media, part of a large advertising group. Howard Glass, the media buying head, had received a glowing recommendation from Doug and invited Jenny in. A week later, she had an offer. She would be an assistant account manager in media placement. Glass told her she would have to learn the trade and that the key to the job would be client relations. The company bought media for a wide range of corporate accounts - from companies in cosmetics to pharmaceuticals to packaged foods. He would put her under a mentor, a company veteran. The salary would be modest at the start, but would be reviewed in six months. If she met expectations, her salary would be increased to the normal range for the job. After that, it would be up to her. It was a big company. Based on what he had heard from Doug Brady, he said he had full confidence in her ability to fit the bill. Jenny was overjoyed.

McGuire's office was in mid-town Manhattan. She could take the train into Union Station every day from Margie's in Stamford, at least for awhile until she found a place in the city. Apartments were expensive in Manhattan, but within a month of starting the job, she found a place in the Tribeca neighborhood on the Lower West Side that was nice, although small. She would end up sharing the two bedroom apartment with a gay male co-worker working on the creative side who was also looking for a place to live in New York. Kevin would turn out to be a great live-in companion - a good person and a great cook, who was also not attracted to women and kept his own sexual life out of sight. Jenny felt safe. The cost of living in Manhattan suddenly became manageable. Jenny and Kevin would become good friends.

She spent the first few months in New York learning her job. With the help of her mentor, she proved the wisdom of being hired and was soon given a number of mid-size accounts to manage. Her salary got bumped up after four months and not six. Kevin's presence lightened the time after work and on weekends. She had no interest in the meantime in a male relationship. Jenny managed to put her angst into periodic remission, but was nevertheless resolved to pressure Washington to intervene for access to her daughters. She kept writing to them every month. She had little confidence in getting anything done with the UN, but was determined to find a way to embarrass the Government of Ghana about their indifference to her plight and that of her daughters.

13

Tim Hurley's return trip to Montreal included a planned two-day layover in Paris for a de-brief with USAID. He would also spend some time with Brian to whom he related what had transpired in Accra. They looked forward to reading new editions of NewsWorld magazine. Brian decided to bring Jenny's treatment by her own government in Ghana to the attention of friends he had at the Paris Embassy. But he knew that circumstances and lines of authority would most likely protect the people in Accra from any serious review of their behavior. He would do it anyway. Neither could know, though, that at the time of their discussion, Jenny was on a flight to New York for the beginning of a very different phase of her life. Whatever intercession Brian or Tim could make on her behalf would most likely fall on deaf ears. She was gone. She had left.

In Montreal, Tim got back into his consulting practice for clients in Canada. Having acquired a taste for international work, he kept his eyes open for opportunities that could interest him and his firm. Canada at that time was providing resources and expertise for economic development projects in many parts of the developing world. Tim soon became aware of many of them. Within a few months of his return, his firm had won a contract to participate in a feasibility study for a major combined mineral extraction and transformation venture in Thailand. It required a consultant to spend two months there, reviewing all of the marketing and financial elements in collaboration with Thai counterparts and the engineers from the prime contractor. It would be the first of many other foreign assignments for Tim Hurley over the next decade.

Like most other people who visit Bangkok, Tim found the city to be a steaming, bustling, noisy, crowded place. It had an energetic night-life. That invariably involved the temptation for foreign men of meeting young, pretty Thai girls in bars, cafes and discos who would ask for modest amounts of money for spending the evening and usually the night with them. Tim quickly became exposed to it. The Thai version of prostitution was quite different from the prostitution of Amsterdam or Las Vegas. The young women involved were neither hardened sex workers whose favors were advertised through the windows of red-light district streets or the gorgeous young women procured through high-priced escort services in Las Vegas. In Bangkok it was simply about young girls from the country wanting to have a good time and going with a man who would take them to a disco or a movie or a restaurant and perhaps to his own hotel room afterwards. They would come away with the equivalent of twenty or thirty dollars. One did not have to go far to see it. There were always two or three pairs of girls having tea or coffee in the hotel coffee shop. The discos and bars along the Bangkok river waterfront were full of those who were available for the evening.

One evening, Tim observed an attractive Thai girl sitting at a table down the aisle with another girl. She was well dressed and had a reserved demeanor. Over the previous month, he had on two occasions met a girl in a disco and spent the night with her. Although Tim was single, did not have a steady companion back in Canada, he nevertheless felt a degree of guilt in participating in the Thai version of prostitution, however mundane and innocuous that version seemed to be. Tim walked down the aisle and asked the two girls if he could sit down with them. The reserved one would consume Tim's attention for the next month and a half.

He came to like her very much. She had said she was Thai Chinese, but looked to speak more French than English. Tim thought that a bit odd. There were not many French speakers in Bangkok. As well, her name was Huang, which Tim learned through counterparts was not a usual Thai name. The young girl came and went. They would make plans to see each the next evening, she would not show up, then appear three days later. She would make it known to Tim in her halting English that she had been to see family. At one point, she disappeared for three weeks. He would find out why three days before his return to Canada. She was not Thai Chinese, she was Lao, a refugee, and had escaped from a displaced persons camp in the north of Thailand. Over two years, she had managed to escape to Bangkok three times. She had been a hair-dresser in Vientiane in that former French colony, was 26 years old and not twenty as she had claimed before, and had been detained in the camp for four years. Her parents were dead. She was on the run from the police - there was no future for her staying in Thailand. At the close of her admission of all this, she broke down and cried. Tim took her into his arms. He felt a suddenly relieved but very scared person who clearly wanted to stay in his embrace. He knew what he would do. He would try to get her out. Over the next two days, he took her to the Canadian, the Australian, and the New Zealand embassies to apply for refugee status. He had to leave Bangkok before the end of the week, but he thought that she could perhaps find a way out of her mess with the help of the embassies. As he did all of this, he learned a lot about the refugee camps, the life inside them and the dangers the refugees faced, particularly faced by young women. It was not a pretty picture. He rented a car on his day off and went on his own to the village where her camp was located. It was not a pretty picture. It would stay in his memory. He left Thailand, hoping what he had started would lead to something for her. He didn't really know if it could. Hundreds of thousands of people were caught in the aftermath of the wars of Southeast Asia and were seeking to get out - to America, Europe, Australia, anywhere far away.

On his way back, Tim had a layover in Paris. He and Brian had lunch and spent time talking about Jenny. Brian had tried to get the US Embassy in Paris to enquire about her. No luck. Said they couldn't do anything. Ghana not part of their territory anyway.

"I don't know where she is or how she is doing. I thought there was going to be something in NewsWorld. Haven't seen anything. Something happened along the way. I thought Jay was going to write the story and get it through," said Tim.

"What a lady. I just wish we could have done more," said Brian.

14

Geoffrey Wilson's decision to not publish Jay Peterson's story had a profound impact on his motivation to continue to ferret out and write on happenings on the continent of Africa. It wasn't the same for him anymore. His relationship with Geoffrey soured. Within six months, he had left Africa and NewsWorld and had taken a job with the NewsMag print media chain in New York. His base would be Manhattan and he would be covering political happenings in Canada as well as the United States. A few weeks after starting the job in 1982, Jay tracked down the Canadian he had met in Accra. The threat of Quebec separation from the rest of Canada had subsided since the defeat of a referendum on the matter in 1980. But there were rumblings of discontent in the aftermath and Tim was tasked with finding out more about it. He needed contacts in the Canadian political world to understand what was going on and Hurley could perhaps help him.

Jay reached Tim at his office. After he explained the reason for his call, Tim wasted no time. "What happened to your project about the American lady? Did you manage to do the story, Jay? The colleague of mine from Paris and I have had no news from or about her. She left Accra. We don't know where she is...Maybe back in the United States, but we don't know. Anything to tell me on that?"

"As I said, I am no longer with NewsWorld. And the Jenny story had a lot to do with it. I won't go any further on the phone, but we could perhaps talk about it when I see you in

Montreal. I do not know where she is. She told me the last day I was there that she was leaving. She was from Toledo, maybe she's there. I don't know, Tim. But I need to get to Montreal for what I am following. Do you think you could help me in getting some meetings with the political crowd up there?" Jay elaborated on what he was looking for.

"Glad to do it. I'm just back from Asia, by the way, and we could talk about that as well – post-Vietnam Southeast Asia. When are you planning to come up?"

"I can be there two weeks from today."

"My London editor canned the whole story, Tim. No guts. I was disgusted. Still am. Turned me off on the European crowd running the international edition out of London. I couldn't work with them anymore. If the story had been in the hands of Ben Crowley, the boss in New York, it would have gone through. He goes for the big story and has confidence in his senior reporters. But it didn't get to him. The guys in London canned it - Ghana is a former British colony after all. Sensitivities about that. And I had no recourse. Geoffrey Wilson, my boss in London, is tight with Crowley. They go back a long ways and Wilson seems to get his way when it comes to the international stuff." Jay Peterson sighed, took a drink from his beer, looked at Tim, then continued.

"It would have been a blockbuster. I was there. It's all true what she told us. I got pulled off the road by the intelligence guy, his goons later came to my room and punched me up. The Embassy clammed up to London when they were doing due diligence on the story. They said they didn't know of anyone with the name of Jennifer or Jenny Sutton Akala who was an American citizen, which only confirmed to me that they wanted to keep Jenny Akala under wraps. It's all true. 'No other corroborating witnesses', Geoffrey said. Bullshit. Tragic situation for a vulnerable lady. Maybe I will see her again. Who knows.......Now this guy from the Parti Quebecois who was a minister in the Quebec government until last year and who I am meeting Wednesday.....tell me about him....."

15

The young man at the Ghanaian UN delegation in New York, Kwasi Kobena, received the call from the embassy in Washington. "We need some surveillance on a woman in New York," said the deputy chief of mission. "She is American and married to a member of the Minister of the Interior's family. She left her husband a couple of years ago and caused trouble for his family. She nearly created an international incident through a magazine correspondent, complaining about her treatment by the Minister's family. As well, she had an affair with our Chief of Intelligence. Caused him to be sacked and put into exile. Dangerous woman." Kobena didn't say anything. The caller continued with what he had to say. "She left the country a few months ago and is now in New York. We are aware of where she works and where she lives. We need someone from the delegation to watch her movements. We need information on what she could be doing to regain custody of her children, who have remained with their father in Yendi. She is obsessed with getting them back. We need to understand who she is speaking to that could be relevant to all this, particularly whatever contacts she is having with the U.S. government here in Washington. We suspect she or someone on her behalf has contacted the State Department. You should have enough resources for that, I would assume. You have a security contingent there. You could use them for this."

The young diplomat who had met Jenny Akala two weeks before and had become sympathetic to her situation sat back in his chair and wondered what he was to do. I can't help her now....despite what she told me, which I am pretty sure is true. Orders to watch her and report. I will do the minimum. I don't think she deserves what has been happening to her, he thought.

Washington, July 1982...

The state department official was on the phone with the aide to the congressman. "We can't help this lady. I know this is the third discussion we have had on this, but we have been advised by the Embassy in Ghana that the problem of this lady is her own fault. The Department has been advised to do nothing about it. A family matter. The lady abandoned her children, then turned out to be somewhat promiscuous in her affairs in Accra and proved bothersome to Embassy officials. She apparently even had a relationship with the head of state security of Ghana, which worried the embassy and caused them to be very careful in how they dealt with her. She left the country without saying goodbye to anyone, including her husband and children. I'm sorry if this is not the information you were seeking." The official paused a moment, then continued. "Please don't call me again on this, Mr. Caraleno. We can't do any more. The file we opened on this is closed unless we get different information from the field. If I can be of assistance to you on other matters, however, please do not hesitate to call."

"You're sure about all that, it seems," responded the congressional assistant. "It is at total variance with what this lady has told us. She is very credible and believable. You say the file is closed. We will respect that, but we are not sure the information you are getting is correct. Congressman O'Brien believes her. Her story could be very injurious to the interests of the United States if it gets out that the U.S. Government abandoned a distressed American mother in such an apparently despicable manner. "

"I'm sorry, but that is all we can do. We have to rely on information from the field and that is what we have," replied the state department official.

"It's all bullshit, Jeremy. The consul there has too much to protect to say anything else. So much for help from my own government. I thank you for your troubles, though. I know you and the Congressman went to bat for me. In the end, it looks like I will have to solve this by myself. Thanks again."

That rat, Keyes. Told Washington a story to cover his butt. No other source to refute it......I'm no closer to my girls.

16

Yendi, two years before

"My little girls, my precious little ones, your mother has left us. She doesn't love you anymore. She has gone home. Your father and I will take care of you. And you will have a new mamma soon. I am sure you will like her."

Efe and Sisi Akala, 7 and 4 years old, looked up at their grandmother. Efe, the oldest, looked at her grandmother for a long moment. Tears welled in her large dark eyes. She said nothing, just looked at her grandmother, trying to comprehend what she was being told. The little one then, with anger directed at her grandmother, blurted out, "I don't want a new Mommy. I want my real Mommy. I want to go with her! I don't like it here!"

"Me too," whispered her older sister. "I don't want a new Mommy."

Sahr Akala and his mother would not allow the girls to speak of their mother in their presence from that point on. Most of the letters Jenny sent her girls were destroyed. The girls never saw any of them, never even knew they existed. For them, their mother was gone. She had abandoned them.

Efe was the curious one. She had the closest relationship with her mother. One morning when she was nine and alone with her father, she asked him. "What happened to Mommy? Why did she leave us? Tell me, Daddy. Please tell me."

"I don't know, my dear. She just left."

With Sahr Akala's second marriage to the young girl from the adjoining clan, the power of the extended Akala family was solidified. Sahr took over his father's construction business and within five years, exercising the family's influence with the government through his mother, turned it into the largest construction firm in northern Ghana. The veterinary practice became secondary. Too much money was being made in construction. The Akala girls received the best education that was available, oddly enough at a Catholic school near one of the principal towns of the north. Muslim rights to having multiple wives did not preclude using Christian institutions for education for the offspring. Grandmother Akala had objected, but Sahr put his foot down. The girls would be educated. Period.

17

New York, 1984

Jenny dove into her work in New York while continuing to write to her daughters every month, looking for opportunities to get them out. It was a hopeless task. She despaired of her inability to make any progress and felt increasingly estranged from her children in spirit as well as presence. It had been over four years since she had seen them. Were they healthy, were they happy, were they doing well in school, did they still fill the room with their smiles? She had no idea.

After two years at the firm, she was presented an opportunity to work on the creative side. She had done well with the clients she had, but confessed to her boss she would like a new challenge. She applied for an executive position and was chosen. The creative side proved to be more stimulating, took her mind off Africa more than the previous job, and she flourished. Within another two years, Jenny Sutton (by this time, she had reverted to her maiden name) had become one of the most valued managers at the firm and had increased her income threefold. Soon after getting the new job, Jenny and Kevin decided they could afford their own Manhattan apartments and, despite being great friends and confidants, they went their separate ways. Jenny found a nice apartment on the Upper East Side and Kevin kept the flat in Tribeca.

Soon after moving in to her own apartment, tragedy struck. Margie died suddenly of a brain aneurism, leaving her husband Bob with their 12 year old son and 10 year old daughter. Jenny spent the first eight weeks after her sister's death living in the house in Connecticut with Bob and the children, commuting into the city every day. After Bob had found a live-in housekeeper during the week, Jenny would nonetheless spend weekends with he and the children. For over a year, she provided a degree of stability to her sister's family and found an outlet for her maternal affections. Bob eventually met someone who became his new partner and replacement mom for his kids. Jenny went back to being a full-time New Yorker, but remained very much attached to her sister's children.

Jenny decided to write Sahr and propose a truce and a way for her to see her children. She wrote him a letter, avoiding any accusations, hoping he would respond positively to her request. He never responded. After three months of no response, Jenny decided to fly to Ghana and drive up to Yendi to make the request in person. She applied for a visitor's visa through the Ghanaian embassy in Washington. The application was turned down. No reason given. It was obvious they had received orders from somewhere on high to refrain from any contact or assistance to the estranged daughter-in-law of the cousin of the Minister of the Interior. Sahr's mother's cousin still had that job and wielded through it much of the power in the government of Ghana.

Washington, September 1986

A woman from the State Department was on the telephone. "Mrs. Sutton, there is no file on you or your children at the Embassy in Accra. Our consular people there could not find anything. There is no record of an Efe or a Sisi Akala ever having been listed as American citizens living in Ghana. Neither is there a record at the Embassy of a Jennifer Sutton Akala having lived in Ghana."

Jenny interrupted before the woman could go any further. "Wait a minute. Four years ago, an aide to Congressman O'Brien of New York was told by someone at State that my situation was a family matter, that I had abandoned my children, that I was even having affairs with men in Ghana. Now you tell me no file exists. What happened to what you had on me four years ago, regardless of whether it was right or wrong?"

"I'm sorry, there is nothing in the files on you or your children, Mrs. Sutton. There is no record of there every having been."

"As if I didn't exist? What about the travel agency job I had in Accra that I told you about when we spoke a few weeks ago? What about that? Did you check that out?" Jenny was incredulous at what she was being told.

"A travel agency in Accra by that name did exist, apparently, but ceased operations in 1983. The consular people at the Embassy could find no one who had been employed there to ask if they knew of you."

"What about the woman I told you about from the Accra office of UK Aid who I had extensive dealings with, Margaret Bishop? Did your people try to check that reference?"

"They did. UK Aid does not have an office in Accra anymore. The management of UK economic development aid was delegated to an independent NGO in 1983. The British High Commission could give no information on the whereabouts of a Margaret Bishop, who you say worked in Accra. I'm sorry, Mrs. Sutton. We have not been able to ascertain the veracity of any of the information you provided us. I am sorry if we cannot go any further."

Jenny was livid. "The passport I had in 1977 shows a stamp of having arrived in Ghana. I was there. I lived there over four years. I had extensive contacts with the Consul-General, who actually badgered me, said he would help with my children, but never did. It is clear to me that, as I have suspected all along, what is going on is an intentional cover-up. The Government of Ghana is complicit in this. What about the Consul-General at the time, Richard Keyes? Has he been contacted about this?"

"Any information about a US Government public servant in a foreign posting, his or her whereabouts, whether he or she was in the continuing employ of the government or otherwise, is not public information. I'm sorry, there is nothing more I can do at this time. If you can give us better, verifiable information that supports your request of us, we may decide to revisit the issue, but I must advise that would be unlikely given what we have done on this to date. Goodbye, Mrs. Sutton."

Keyes. Covered up everything. I'm going to have to go there somehow. Have to find a way to get in.

New York, 1988

One evening seven years after her arrival in New York and six months after returning to the city full-time from helping with her sister's family, Jenny had dinner with a man she had met a few weeks earlier at a cocktail party. He told her he had been driving the past two years in the grueling Paris to Dakar off-track road race. Jenny expressed interest and asked him to tell her the experience of it all. Paul Russo explained what the race was all about. He had a special Peugeot 205 outfitted for it with the aid of a couple of corporate sponsors. Before the dinner was out, he had asked Jenny if she wanted to be his rider in the next edition, six months hence. She accepted right away. The race didn't come close to Ghana, but it would be fun. She cleared the use of vacation time for it with her boss the next day and plans were made.

In the meantime, Brian Maxwell met a lady who introduced herself as Margaret Bishop at a seminar on international development in London. They quickly discovered they had a common connection to Ghana. Margaret said that she was working in a special program on determining best practices in international education development at the University of London. She had worked extensively in Ghana, India and Nepal before leaving the government aid organization, UK Aid, a few years previous. Brian asked her if she knew of a Jenny Sutton Akala, an American lady he had met in Ghana at about the same time as Margaret said she had been stationed there. She replied that she did know the woman, that she had come close to financing her school for girls upcountry and that they had been friends. She said she still had the American woman's parrot, Buckeye, that was left to her when the lady decided to suddenly leave Ghana. "By the way, Brian, what is a Buckeye? Never bothered to look up the name, but have always wondered where it came from."

"It is a flower, but also the symbol, nickname if you wish, of a college football team in Ohio. They call themselves the Buckeyes. Jenny Akala was from Ohio. Toledo."

"Oh," replied the English lady with a touch of wry humor. "I'll have to tell Buckeye he descends from football."

"What happened to Jenny, Margaret? Where is she now? Do you know?"

"She went back to the States. New York. She wrote me six months or so after getting there. She had just come out of a depression and had found work with an advertising agency. She wrote to see if I had any news of her children. I had to tell her that I did not. Such a tragic story. She couldn't get any help, even from her own government when she was in Ghana. I don't know if she succeeded in resolving anything from the outside."

"I know her story. She told me I was one of the first persons she unloaded her situation to after she had been thrown out of the home by her husband. I have always wondered what happened to her. A buddy of mine, a Canadian, tried to help her, but lost track as well. Do you have any idea of how to reach her?"

"Well, I do remember that the company she went to work for was called McGuire, McGuire Advertising or something like that. I remember the name because my mother was a McGuire. The name stuck. But I don't have an address or a number. The letter from Jenny was seven years ago. I don't think I kept it."

"That may be enough, Margaret. There is a McGuire Media in New York. Maybe that is where she worked and maybe she's still there. I'm glad we met. We should stay in touch. We both work in the development field to begin with."

The day after his encounter with Margaret Bishop. Brian was on the phone to Boston where Tim now lived and worked. "Tim, I think I know where our lady from Toledo could be. It's worth a try. You're in New York often enough. She may be there."

"What makes you think she is in New York?" replied Tim.

Tim Hurley placed the call to McGuire Media the next day. "Could I speak with Jennifer Sutton Akala please?"

"We have a Jennifer Sutton, but I am not aware of a Jennifer Sutton Akala working here. Could the person you are trying to reach be Jennifer Sutton?"

"Yes, of course. Ms. Sutton was married to a man named Akala at one time. Please put me through to her, if you could."

"Jenny, this is Tim Hurley. The last time we spoke was the evening at your house in Accra."

There was a moment of silence at the other end of the line. "Tim. The Canadian. Yes, of course. How are you?"

"I'm fine, Jenny. I am in New York next week and I wondered if we couldn't have lunch or dinner. I must say I have never forgotten your predicament. Do you have your children with you? "

"No, Tim, I do not have them with me. It has been a very painful odyssey. But, yes, I would be glad to see you again. How about Tuesday evening, if you are in town as you say? There is a great Italian restaurant on 54th Street halfway between 5th and 6th avenues. You can't miss it. We could meet there. They always manage to find a table for me."

"Good. I'll find it. See you there at 6?"

"Very good, Tim. See you then. Bring news of Brian if you could. Still in contact with him?"

"Oh yes, still in touch with Brian. See you next next."

The following Tuesday, Tim Hurley was walking along 5th Avenue near 54th Street when he saw the tall, dark-haired lady across the street, striding briskly in the same direction. It was her. It could not be anybody else. He cried out to her, their eyes met over the slow-moving traffic. Tim crossed the street, the two of them hugged, then proceeded to the restaurant a block away.

"What happened to you, Jenny? When I left, you were going to meet with Jay Peterson."

Jenny replied, "I did meet with Jay. He said he would write a story on my situation for the magazine. It never appeared, as far as I know. It was a mistake, my telling it all to him. The intelligence people knew all about our meeting. Had me fired from my job. I couldn't stand it any longer. I decided to leave Ghana, work to get my kids back some other way."

She told Tim of her exit, her despair in the early days back home, her efforts to get the U.S. government to help to no avail. She told him of her one-way correspondence with her husband and the refusal of the government there to give her a visa, as well as her intent to get into the country any way she could.

"Still a hell for you. Many years now you haven't seen your kids."

"I don't know what they are like, how they look.....They are so far away from me.....I wonder if they will ever try to find me, to even try to contact me. They are fifteen and twelve now. I can't believe they have forgotten me. This has obviously consumed me. I can't hold that back. I try to do things, to think of something else, get my mind elsewhere, but it's always there. My husband and his people have certainly painted me as a witch, as the mother who abandoned her family. It's entirely probable that they tell people that Sahr's new wife was taken only after I left, a replacement for the good of the children. The U.S. Government and the Government of Ghana, for different reasons, have made me disappear. For both of them, I did not live there, my kids are not mine, there is no record of a Jenny Sutton Akala in their files. I have not given up, though, Tim. I will find a way."

She paused, then took the discussion in another direction. "What happened to Jay and the article he was to write? I thought he would do it. What happened?"

"He did submit it. Got turned down by his managing editor in London. Not enough corroborating evidence, apparently. Caused him to leave NewsWorld. Was very bitter about it. He felt he had let you down. He's in New York by the way, with another magazine covering political affairs. I think he would like to see you if he knew where you were."

"Let him know I'm here, in the city, Tim. Here's my card. I would like to hear from him what happened about the story."

Changing the subject again, Jenny proceeded to tell Tim of her plans for the Paris - Dakar road race. "I know a lot about that," said Tim. "I spent two years managing a development project in Mali. The race came through the bush village where our base of operations was. Many participants would stop for the night before continuing on to the last leg across Senegal into Dakar. They pitched tents next to their vehicles for a quick night's sleep but not before drinking a few beers with us Canadians in the project compound. We had a hut we converted into a bar. Had to keep it pretty low key. Sensitive subject in that traditionally Muslim area of the country. But most people ended up knowing about the Canadian watering hole in the dusty mud-hut village. Anyway, the place.....everybody would be covered in dust and grime. There was no shower facility for them anywhere on the trail or at their stopover points. With the grime and the crud, they would nevertheless get into the beer which we had en masse and get into song. A Brit got up on the bar in our makeshift saloon one year and belted out a crude version of Midnight Rambler of Rolling Stones fame. French guy followed with a rendition of La Bohème by Aznavour. Showed for all of us the difference between the Brits and the French. Rockers and lovers."

"Come on. You mean to tell me I'll be going through a place in the middle of nowhere in Mali where you spent two years? Our African connection continues," replied Jenny.

"Let me finish on the place where I was, Jenny. When you get to the village of the stopover, called Nioro du Sahel, find a man by the name of Seydou Touré. He is a very enterprising fellow. Knows West Africa like the back of his hand. Former Malian army officer. Tough guy, but very human and likable in his own way. I think he could perhaps help you get into Ghana if you want to try it again without encountering any border checkpoints or any of that. Knowing him, I think he would be glad to try to help you. He was great for us Canadians when I was there. He will expect some compensation to do it, but he is honest. Seydou Touré. Has a vehicle repair shop in the center of town. Worth a try. Mention my name of course."

"I will do just that. Thank you, Tim. This is quite something. Quite incredible. Wow. Seydou Touré....have to write it down."

"Maybe it will help you. Let's hope it does." At that moment, a waiter approached their table, they ordered glasses of wine and looked at menus. After ordering, Tim continued with the discussion, "In the meantime, Jenny, what have you been doing here? I must say you look prosperous."

"I may look prosperous, Tim, but whatever you see hides my underlying grief. I have drowned my predicament in work and in looking after other people here. I volunteer time on weekends for a shelter for battered women in Harlem. Fundraising and some counseling. I must be the only white face there, but I enjoy it. I may think I have personal problems but some of the people I come across have far worse situations than mine. During the week, I run much of the creative side of McGuire Media now. I make a very good living at it, but there is that big hole in my life. I would give this up in a minute to be back with my children. They are growing up and I am not part of it. My life is moving on and theirs is too. I've never really understood my husband's obstinacy on this. He wasn't like that the first years. Something happened. A mystery. Couldn't be just his mother and her machinations."

18

January 1989

It was a crazy trip down through France, on a ship across the Mediterranean, then down through the desert of Algeria, into northern Mali, past Timbuktu, then west across the sub-Sahara. They carried extra fuel cans attached to the back, stacked four extra tires on the roof, had an iron grill added on the front. The Peugeot 250 looked like a Mad Max road racer, with Valvoline and Delco decals on the hood and each side. Paul Russo was a good driver, this Paris-Dakar race was his third, and he knew what to avoid. One, stay out of the dust trail of whoever was in front. The most important things was to be able to see what was in front of you. Hitting a gully at full speed could break an axle. Two, don't press it. "Keep the powder dry," he would say. Jenny was in charge of measuring distance and watching out for other vehicles, ahead, off to the side, and behind.

They raced by herds of goats that scattered off, by Tuareg nomads in black by their tents in the distance, by caravans of camels, past dusty towns of mud huts and minarets, swerved to avoid gullies, ruts and rocks in the road, all rolling along in a swirling cloud of dust as fast as they could. Tank trucks, motorcycles, pick-up trucks and other modified cars like Paul's Peugeot raced along, not all following the same track. The object was to get to Dakar first. Some went through Timbuktu and Nioro, others went by further north or south. The most direct route after Algeria and the north of Mali was through Nioro. There was a semblance of a road and there was the camp of

Canadians. Some didn't care to stop. Depended on the time taken to that point. But to keep going in the dark asked for trouble. Most people stopped, pitched their tent, slept a few hours, then continued on at first light.

Paul and Jenny were making good time and found the dusty village around seven in the evening. It would be dark in an hour. Jenny immediately went into the center of the town to see if she could find the man Tim suggested she meet. A young boy when asked if the shop he was in front of belonged to a Monsieur Touré, nodded and pointed to a man sitting twenty feet away, by himself, at a metal table with a couple of rickety chairs. He appeared to half expect being asked for. Seeing the boy point his way, he rose and approached the woman covered in dust who had parked her very dirty race car in front of his shop.

"Monsieur, are you Seydou Touré?" she asked the man who was approaching her.

"Yes, that is me. *Qu'est-ce que je peut faire pour vous?* Forgive my English. What can I do for you, Madame?" said the tall, lean ruddy-faced man.

"I am a friend of Tim Hurley, a Canadian, who I believe you know. As you can probably see from the car, I am a participant in the Dakar race. Monsieur Hurley suggested I try to find you and speak to you while here."

"*Pourquoi, Madame?* Why do you want to speak to me?"

"Do you have a moment? Could we have a cola or something from the cafe? Tim suggested you may be able to help me."

"*Certainement*, Madame. I liked Mister Hurley very much. If he believes I can help a friend of his, I am willing to listen."

Jenny proceeded to explain to Seydou Touré her need, that she could require transportation and assistance to get into Ghana without going through a border checkpoint, at a time to be determined. She told him of her children who had been taken from her and her wish to find a way to see them and possibly get them out. They were girls, 16 and 13 years of age.

"When do you want to do this?" asked the former commando. "It is now January. The best time to cross into Ghana would be before the rainy season which is in July and August. What are your plans? I could do it with you. It would not be a problem. But you must let me know when."

"I am not sure yet. I wanted to meet you first and see if it was possible. You tell me it is. I believe you. Monsieur Hurley has a great deal of respect for you. I must first finish the race, return to America, and determine a good time to come back. I would like to do it this year, but it may not be possible. I will let you know."

"*Très bien*, Madame. I have a telephone in Bamako. This is the number. Call me when you have decided when to do it. The person who will answer, my nephew, will take your number in America and let me know you have called. I will call you at the first opportunity. When we do this, you could go to Bamako. We would leave for Ghana from there. I have a few different routes we could take."

"What would be the cost?" asked Jenny before leaving the cafe.

After a moment of thought, the man responded. "Five thousand American dollars. Everything included. *Il y a des risques.* There are risks with what we will be doing, Madame. *Ça va?"*

"*Ça va. A bientôt, Monsieur.*" Jenny had no problem with the amount. She had expected it to be higher.

"*A bientôt,* Madame."

Jenny left the center of the village and found the Canadian compound on the outskirts where by that time more than forty vehicles were parked along the road. Crews could be seen cooking on portable stoves and milling about around small fires. It was a beautiful cloudless evening with the promise of a cool night. There was a hut on the edge of the compound where race people were congregating. Jenny parked the Peugeot, got out to find Paul, and found him in the hut singing along with two other thoroughly filthy bearded men the lyrics to Mack the Knife, all three with beers in hand, with people clapping as they finished.

"Did you find your man, Jenny?"

"Found my man. We're good. Ready to roll tomorrow. What do we have to eat?"

"Those guys from Montreal who are serving the beer are here on some project. They have invited whoever is in the bar and hasn't eaten already over to their trailer camp for lamb burgers and rice and all the tomatoes we can eat from their vegetable garden. What do you say?"

"I say we accept," replied Jenny. "Think they could throw in a shower along with the food?"

Jenny thought she could organize things to be back in Mali in a few months for the trip to Yendi. It scared her. She didn't think she was ready. She put it off. Sent Seydou a note. *L'année prochaine, Seydou.* I will let you know.

19

Washington, February 1990

Mustafa Korafa had spent eight years as warden of the prison. He was an angry man and had been for a long time. The best years of his career had been wasted, all because of a woman. His latest request for a transfer to something else in the service of Ghana finally led to an offer for another posting. For head of security at the embassy in Washington. The military chief of staff put in a good word for his reinstatement. It was not an entirely altruistic motive on his part. Korafa was dangerous. He knew a lot. He would be less trouble in Washington than if he were back in Accra.

Korafa had paid his dues. But Washington.... He could not believe his luck. He could begin to exact his revenge, at least part of it. The Akala part could come later. Upon arriving, Korafa virtually immediately began to track down the whereabouts of Jenny Sutton Akala. He knew she was in America, but did not know where. The Embassy knew, though. She was in New York. They had an address in Manhattan from contacts with her five years before. The file showed her attempt to obtain a visa to visit Ghana. It was turned down. As well, an employee of the UN delegation had been ordered to keep tabs on her for awhile. As recently as a month before, the file said that Madame Akala lived at an address on Duane Street in the New York neighborhood of Tribeca.

In his first few weeks in Washington, Korafa kept his head down, stayed in the capital, and ingratiated himself with the Ambassador before adventuring to New York. Quickly, though, he learned where Jenny worked in addition to where she lived. He decided he would have her killed, but not before some injection of fear. He would not do the ultimate deed itself. He needed the Washington job and killing someone in America without the FBI discovering who did it did not have a high degree of probability. It would be someone on contract, but one who would not cost him anything. An old undercover assassin from his secret service days back home who had moved to London years before was now working as a taxi driver in Miami. Korafa found him easily enough. The embassy was keeping tabs on him. It would not even cost Korafa any money. He had a file on the man that he would divulge if he refused to do the deed. The former intelligence operative had killed a politician in Ghana in 1980 and had left the country. The government had been livid at the killing, but the crime had never been solved. Korafa knew about it and had proof of the man's guilt. After being contacted in Miami, the man acquiesced to the murder scheme. He had been a killer ever since his youth. He knew Korafa had an incriminating photograph of his entering the politician's home that night years ago. He was sure Korafa would use it if he did not go along with murdering the American woman. Korafa had nothing to lose and everything to gain by exposing him. On the other hand, if he killed the woman, he and Korafa would both have something to hide. It was a fair exchange of reasons to cooperate. In the meantime, Korafa would put a bit of fear in Madame Sutton Akala. It could backfire, but he needed to do it. She had ruined his career.

Korafa drove to New York early one Saturday morning and found his way to a housing project in the Bronx. Sitting on a bench on the periphery of the playground, he observed a small group of young men gathered on the fenced-in basketball court fifty yards away. The one with the gold chain. Looks to be the leader. The former intelligence agent dressed in jeans, black hoodie and sunglasses approached the court and got the attention of the kid with the chain. He motioned him to come over. The young man hesitated, spread his hands, then said, "What do you want, asshole?"

"Maybe a deal for you. Do you want to talk or pass up a good deal?" replied Korafa.

"Alright, what's it about?"

"Need you to come over here."

The young sauntered over towards Korafa. "OK, buddy, what's the so-called good deal?"

"I need a job done."

"What kind of job?" replied the young man.

"Scare somebody. No theft, no killing, just scare them."

"How much we talking about?"

"Five thousand dollars. Two before, three after. I get you in to the place, and get you out. Need you and somebody else - maybe one of your buddies over there."

"You a cop?"

"No, not a cop."

"OK. Five big ones for scaring somebody. Whew. Tell me more, man."

"Only if you agree to do it. If you tell anybody about this, I will know. Won't be nice. Can we do a deal?"

"Probably, but I gotta know more. Sounds too good to be true. Sounds like a set-up."

"Not a set-up."

Mustafa Korafa checked out apartment 310 from across the street. Before picking the lock on the back door, he put a stocking over his head with holes for eyes and mouth. He had determined the previous week that the alarm connected to the door was not functioning. That surprised him, but it had simplified his plan. He checked again. Alarm not working. He had entered the block from the alley an hour before to see where apartment 310 was. The boys could get in. He proceeded to check out the location of the apartment in relation to the street. From the door across the street, he saw a woman's silhouette cross in front of the window. She's there. Time to put a bit of fear into Madame Akala. He motioned to the boys down the street at the corner of the alleyway to stay put. He waited until the lights went off in the apartment. A little after midnight, he gave the signal and the boys in black head stockings entered the block through the door at the back; the door was still ajar as Korafa had left it. They proceeded to the third floor. The plan was to enter Jenny's apartment, find her, gag and tie her up, scare her thoroughly with a knife, then leave. Being careful to avoid anyone as they mounted the steps, they quickly picked the lock of Apartment 310 and used powerful wire cutters to cut the chain on the inside through the opening. The boys entered the apartment only to find two men cuddled up in the dark as they watched television with half-finished glasses of wine on the coffee table. One was wearing a wig, lipstick and net stockings. The other was in a silk negligee. They looked with open mouths at the black clad hooded men who had just entered the apartment. No woman. Two gays. The boys quickly turned and left.

They met at the corner of the alleyway. The taller of the two brandished the knife in the face of Korafa. "Asshole. There was no woman in there. Two fags cuddled up, drinking wine. The cash. The cash, man. We're out of here."

"Two gay guys? What? You sure? Apartment 310. There was a woman in the window an hour ago."

"Fag dressed as one, buddy. Cash! Not our fault you fucked up."

The imbeciles at the Delegation. She was supposed to be living here. Have to get away. "Sorry. Here it is. Run. They will have the police here."

Kevin had immediately called 911. Two black men, as far as he could tell, entering the apartment with a lock pick and wire cutters, then quickly leaving.

The alleyway was a dead-end with a wall at the end. They had to exit into the street. They quickly removed their stocking caps and threw them in a trash bin as they rounded the corner on to Broadway. A police car siren came closer. Korafa hailed a taxi coming down Broadway and managed to escape the police cordon that soon took shape. The boys blended into the crowd and made their way down a side street before the police could seal off the area.

Kevin told Jenny of the break-in the next morning at the office. Suspecting the break-in had to do more with her than with her former roommate, she called the FBI, believing the perpetrators could be related to her problems with Ghana. Korafa had made a mistake. He put his stocking cap on too close to entering the building in the back. There was a concealed security camera on the outside wall near the door. Within twenty-four hours, the FBI had identified the man putting on the hood. Two other men entering could not be identified. FBI had pictures of all foreign operatives in their files. The match was unmistakable. The man with the stocking cap was Mustafa Korafa, former head of the secret service in Ghana, and for a little over eight weeks the head of security at the country's embassy in Washington. The FBI informed the State Department and before the end of the week, State had requested Korafa's departure from the United States. At a meeting, Ghana's ambassador was shown the video of Korafa putting on a stocking cap and entering the building on Duane Street in New York, along with the recording of the 911 call from the resident of the building.

Before getting on the plane to leave the country, Korafa managed to reach the taxi man in Miami and in a dialect of Akan, the main language of Ghana, gave him the order to proceed. By the time the translation to English was made, the plane with Korafa on it was out of United States airspace and out of the jurisdiction of American authorities. The order to 'carry out the deed' nevertheless led to the interception by the FBI in Miami of the erstwhile assassin. After extensive questioning which ended up revealing nothing of the true nature of the arrangement he had made with Korafa, he was released from police custody, but not before the US Immigration Service had ordered his deportation. Having dual Ghanaian and British citizenship, the man elected to go to the United Kingdom, with the intent of disappearing completely from the attention of the Ghanaian secret service.

"You fool. Still pursuing the American woman. How stupid. The Ambassador could not believe you would stoop to something like this. Major embarrassment, Korafa. Fortunately for you, the American media have not picked it up. I can't protect you anymore..... Major, you are being de-commissioned from the Armed Forces. You have brought it upon yourself. I request you turn in your service revolver and your uniform before the end of the day. You will continue to be paid your salary for another two months. After that, you are on your own. And...I advise you to be careful." The military chief of staff turned and left. He knew that the now former Major Mustafa Korafa knew a lot of the goings-on of the current government from his days as head of intelligence, but he had little choice. He had gone too far. The Ambassador to the United States was a high school classmate of the veterinarian from Yendi. The idiot. He should have known that. He was the head of intelligence.

20

Bamako, Mali, April 1990

Jenny got off the plane from Paris, went quickly through customs and immigration, retrieved her bag and found Seydou waiting for her at the exit.

"Bonjour, Madame. Bienvenu de nouveau au Mali. Welcome back to Mali."

"Bonjour, Monsieur Touré. Happy to be back. Thank you for waiting for me on all of this."

"I understood, Madame. It could be difficult for you. Rushing it last year before the rainy season would have not been wise," replied Seydou.

"I appreciate your patience with me," said Jenny. After a pause, looking at Seydou, she continued, "I hope we can accomplish what we are setting out to do."

"We shall see. We must go over the plan. We leave tomorrow morning. We can discuss it all at breakfast tomorrow. In the meantime, we will have a meal this evening with my sister's son and his wife. I have reserved a room for you at the Hotel de l'Amitié. We will go there now. I will pick you up at 7 pm and we will proceed to my nephew's house. No worries. It will be a relaxing evening. Ali and his wife are wonderful company and Madame is a splendid cook. We will not talk of our destination. I will say it is Gao, by the way. An old friend of yours is there. *N'est ce pas?* By the way, Madame, you have your tourist visa for Burkina Faso? Everything is in order? I have mine."

"I have my visa. On that, everything is in order."

"Very good."

Jenny and Seydou had a pleasant evening with Ali and his wife. The sound of the cicadas in the trees reminded her of evenings spent in the yard behind her little house on the lane in Accra ten years before.

The next morning, Seydou and Jenny took to the road for Ouagadougou, the capital of Burkina Faso, and then south into Ghana. Seydou had been up since 5 AM, loading up the Land Rover with water, food, camping equipment and jerry cans of extra fuel. "I have brought camping equipment, Madame. Rest assured. There are two tents, not one," said the man as they drove away from the hotel.

"Merci, Monsieur Toure. You are an honorable man," said the lady, smiling as she looked at the man next to her behind the wheel.

"It is close to 1300 kilometers to Yendi by the shortest route using the best roads, Madame. At best, we could arrive in Yendi tomorrow evening. Before we get to the border of Burkina with Ghana, however, we will have to go off road and proceed in the dark with our lights off. It will be half-moon, so it should not be too dark for us to see our way. We will cross the line in the middle of the night. In that area, there are few manned stations. I am not sure about patrols. We will have to choose high ground for visibility and proceed slowly with no lights. We should be able to do it with no problem, provided we are careful. If we are stopped while in Burkina, it could be trouble, but we have our visas. I would explain you are an American and you wanted to take pictures of wild life in the bush, that the southern part of the country was good for that. I am your driver and bodyguard. That should be sufficient, but the police would most likely require us to regain the road if we were stopped. Assuming we are not stopped and we get across without trouble, after a few kilometers in Ghana, we can stop and sleep for a few hours before continuing. We can find the road down to Yendi ten or fifteen kilometers past the border. It is four hours from there to Yendi. We should get there mid-day, two days from now. If we are stopped in Ghana, it will be another matter. We will have to avoid that at all costs. We will have no right to be in the country. I have brought a set of Ghana license plates for the vehicle to avoid attention. With Mali plates, we would be very suspect. We will have to avoid arousing suspicion."

"I am in your hands, Monsieur," replied Jenny, "but I am aware of the risks. I need to do it. I can't go on the way I have. I will explain to you as we drive."

Over a long stretch of the road, Jenny explained her situation, why she was doing all this, providing far more information to Seydou than the essentials she had given him the year before.

"I can understand, Madame," said Seydou. "I have six children. They are all grown up now, except for the baby who is sixteen. Neither I nor my wife could have born being separated from them. It would have been intolerable. I have thought about that. It is one of the reasons I agreed to help you. It is a dishonor to the men of Africa what your husband has done to you. I am not a fool to believe anyone would believe I am helping you to do what I can to re-establish the honor of African men, but I believe there is some element of motivation for me in that." Seydou paused, then continued. "I will tell you a story that will perhaps illustrate the difficulty that men in Africa have towards their women. It is actually something that our friend Tim and I experienced a few years ago when he was here. An attitude that will take a long time to change."

"The project Tim and I were working on at the time involved drilling a new well in the middle of a village not far from Nioro. The village in question had no surface water in its immediate vicinity. Women had to walk something like six or seven kilometres to the nearest reliable well and then back every day with gourds filled with water for cooking and other needs. The project's hydro geologist had, however, discovered an abundance of water at 50 metres below the village. He, Tim and I went there one day to announce there soon would be a well in the center of the village. We met with a group of elders. On behalf of the project team, I announced that we would be starting the following week on drilling the well that we could put up within a few yards of where they were sitting."

"Well, there was an eruption from the men gathered in front of us. I should have known. Every man in the group proceeded to yell at once. The atmosphere was very heated. I had to take the Canadians off to the side and explain. With the existing well so far away, the women of the village were gone all day. The men said they had peace and quiet and this had been the everyday environment for them for years. What we were announcing was the end of all that. There was no way they were going to put up with having the well in the middle of town. Tim and I had to find a solution. Another part of the project plan for the region was to build storage bins for grain. The farmers in the area, many of whom were there that day, needed them. We came up with a proposal to save face for everyone. The hydro geologist said the water table below the village stretched out a kilometer or so to the west of the village. We returned to the men assembled and told them we would put the well a half-kilometre from the centre of the village and if the elders accepted that, we would build the grain storage facilities after all. If they insisted on the status quo regarding the well, we would build the storage bins in the next village. They would have nothing. *À prendre ou à laisser*. Take it or leave it. They accepted it, but were not happy. An example, Jenny, of the male attitude toward our women here."

The Malian continued. "I must ask you, though, Madame. What will you do if your children refuse to come with you? It has been a long time. Have you prepared for that? It is a difficult question, but I must ask it."

"I don't know," sighed Jenny. "I haven't even thought of it. I don't know what I would do if that were the case. Thinking about it now, as you ask the question, I think it could very well destroy me."

"It may be painful to consider, but we must think of the consequences of that possibility. We could be exposed and have difficulty leaving the country. I have thought about it since our first discussion. I have a friend in a senior position in the Ghana police. He owes me a favor. I saved his life twenty years ago. We may have to cash in the debt. Let us make sure we don't have to go that far. If we find your girls, let us hope they want to join you, Madame." Seydou Touré looked over at Jenny Sutton in the passenger seat and flashed a nervous smile.

"Oui, Monsieur. I really don't know what I will do if they don't."

"Well, our plan is to have them be aware of your presence in Yendi; hopefully, bring them to you. It will be up to you to convince them to come with us. You know the village there and the house where you and your family lived. If your daughters are there, I can pass for someone looking for their father or a member of the family for whatever reason. It will be my challenge to find a way to see them and ask them if they want to see their mother. I will say you are there and I could bring them to you. If they accept and the way is clear, I bring them to you. Then, it is up to you. They come with us or they stay. If they stay, we may be in trouble. If they come with us, we leave immediately. They will have to understand that. If they don't even want to see you, I will have to make an escape from wherever I am. A lot of ifs, Madame."

"Yes, Seydou, many ifs. I don't know if it will be possible to separate them from my husband or if it is even possible for you to approach them. The plan may have to be very different. If they are in school or elsewhere outside the home, you or I could conceivably approach them fairly easily. If the only option is to get to them in the home, it becomes very problematic. It may turn out the safest way would be to find a third person in the village to pass a message to them that I am in the vicinity and want to see them, but that they must not tell anyone."

"Let's find them first. Then we decide what to do," said Seydou.

"This is crazy. Absolutely crazy, Seydou. Back in Ohio, where I am from, people would call this a wild goose chase. But I must go through with it," sighed Jenny as they drove along in the searing heat.

Seydou Touré and Jenny crossed from Mali into Burkina Faso without incident; the road to the capital, a part of the Trans-Sahelian Highway network, was paved and they made good time. They found a small hotel in one of the villages leading into Ouagadougou and spent the night there before continuing south into Ghana. In late afternoon the following day Seydou stopped in a village fifteen kilometers from the border, announcing to Jenny they would have to kill some time and wait for darkness before going off road and navigating the area.

Seydou had not noticed any police vehicles on the road that day or in the village where they stopped for a meal. There would be for sure if they stayed on the road and were approaching the border. *"Ça va bien, Madame.* No police. Let us hope our luck extends into Ghana."

"Very well. I am in your hands," responded Jenny as she sipped her tall glass of minted tea on the shaded terrace of the roadside restaurant.

"The next segment of the voyage will be more difficult," said Seydou. "The bush. There will be gullies and hills that we will go through and over with hidden rocks that we must avoid. It will be rough. According to the map, we will have to cross two river beds. I hope the sand in the bottom will not be too soft for us to cross. If we are stuck in sand, it may be difficult for us to get out of it. I will do my best. The Land Rover is built for this sort of terrain. We shall see. The rougher the terrain, the less likely we will encounter patrols."

The Land Rover meandered its way in the moonlight of the African night through outcrops of rocks, across river beds with soft bottoms, encountered a family of baboons shrieking in the night. They awoke a herd of cattle and its nomad herder, with Seydou waving to him in the distance, hoping the man thought he was police or an official of some kind, then proceeded as far as possible from there to stop, pitch their tents, and get a few hours sleep before daybreak. The ground was dry everywhere. Small trees and bushes dotted the landscape of dry river beds and an occasional dusty track used by herders. They kept as much as possible to the bush as they neared the border.

At dawn, they were back on their way, found the road from Paga to Yendi which was two hundred seventy-five kilometers further. Seydou checked the road from a hill overlooking the highway with binoculars for sight of police or any other vehicles. With no one in sight in the early morning haze, they took to the highway, stopping for petrol and replenishment of water bottles halfway to Yendi.

Yendi, mid-day.

"The house is in the eastern part of the town, left of the road. Go further. I will show you where to turn." Jenny had put on a hijab. They could not afford to have her recognized in her old village, although it had been over a decade since she had lived there.

The dust-covered gray vehicle meandered slowly through the town.

"Turn left at the next intersection, Seydou," said Jenny as they drove down the main street of the town, virtually deserted in the heat of mid-day. "The house and the veterinary clinic if it still exists will be slightly up the hill to the left over there," pointing to a hill with a few trees on its upper slopes a half-mile or so away. There should still be an area off the side of the complex where there are trees and where we can park to observe the house. The place I am thinking of is about four hundred meters from the house. We will be able to see what activity is there, vehicles, perhaps even the occupants. The girls should be around if their schooling is close by."

"Are you nervous, Madame?" asked Seydou as they turned up the road towards her former home.

"Yes, I am. It has been a long time. I have spent ten years in a sort of emotional exile, Seydou. I don't know how this is going to go. I will be relying on you."

"Hmmm. I see the house and yes, over there the place you suggest we can use to observe." There were a few cinderblock houses with walled courtyards on the lane leading to the observation area. There was no traffic on the lane. Not a soul in sight. Seydou parked the vehicle under a huge tree, keeping it from view from up the hill and the house Jenny said had been her family's home. The whole area was dry as bone. Brown everywhere. The rains would be coming, and everything would eventually turn to shades of green, but the rains were still a few weeks away.

"Stay here, Madame. Do not get out of the vehicle," said Seydou. "I am going to walk up the hill, at least a certain distance, and maybe I can see what is up there, the people who are there, if anyone is outside. There is a small house over to the right. I will make it look like I am walking to the house."

Jenny watched as Seydou walked up the hill towards the smaller house on the slope. Three quarters of the way up, Seydou turned, stooped to pick something up, then walked back to the Land Rover parked under the tree.

"An older couple are up there, Madame. I saw them. There are chickens in the yard - we can't see them from here because of the crest of the hill, just before the house. There is a donkey tied in the back. The old man looked like he was bringing water to the donkey. The older woman was sweeping the terrace that has a short wall around half its perimeter. There is no evidence of any children. The building in the back looks like a stable. It does not look like a functioning veterinary hospital or anything like that."

"What you are telling me, Seydou, is that my husband and the children don't live there anymore. Sahr would never have chickens roaming free in the yard with a donkey tied up to the house. Maybe it is one of his father's brothers and his wife that live there now. But it can't be my family. It is clear to me. They have moved somewhere else." Jenny was silent for a moment, then continued as she looked up the hill. "They are still in this town somewhere. It is the base of the Akala family. Everything they have in terms of influence and power is here. Have to think of what we can do......"

"I will ask someone about the animal doctor. We will go back to the cafe on the road. You will get down on the seat in the back. No one should see you," said Seydou as he started the motor and turned to find the road leading outside of town.

Jenny kept herself laid out on the back seat as Seydou entered the cafe. In the local dialect he had gained when he had worked in Ghana in his youth, he asked the cafe owner where the town veterinarian lived. He told the man he was helping a herder with some sick goats he had come across a few kilometers from the village. The man told him where the vet lived and had his practice.

"I know where your husband has his practice now. It is on the other side of town from where we were, in a grove surrounding a spring. Madame, you must stay hidden. Keep the hijab to cover your head as well." Seydou found a hill not far from the animal clinic, parked the vehicle, and took out his binoculars. As he was looking, he described what he saw to Jenny in the back. "Very big house, Madame. No sign of children or young people...your daughters are no longer small children. I see no activity. Let us wait a while. Maybe someone will emerge from the house or the building that looks like it is the animal clinic."

Ten minutes later, Seydou murmured softly. "I think I am seeing your husband, Madame. Tall, thin man in white coat walking from the house to the animal building. He has stopped. He is looking up the road that leads down to his house and the grove of trees that surround it. There is a pick-up truck in the lane. Akala Construction is written on the side. Do you want to see him, Madame?"

"Yes, pass me the binoculars." She had almost said no. She had resolved over the years since leaving Yendi that she never wanted to see Sahr again. But, it was necessary here. Jenny rose up in the back seat, made sure the hijab concealed most of her face, and looked through the binoculars. "Yes, that's him. That is my husband. My former husband," she said in a low voice masking her emotions as she observed the man who had so betrayed her. "No sign of the girls. Let's stay here for awhile and keep watching." Jenny kept the binoculars on the man in the distance. I can't believe he did this to me, she thought. What got into him? Such a sweet man. Gentle. Had his heart on his sleeve. I loved him. Truly loved him. She turned away and gave the binoculars back to Seydou.

"Madame, we can't stay here too long. We will be noticed. Where we are parked does not appear to be a place where one would normally stay parked very long. It is the only place that I can see that allows a clear view of the complex down the hill. But more than another thirty minutes here will invite curiosity."

"You are right. Have to think of some way to find out if the girls are here or away somewhere else," Jenny replied.

Fifteen minutes later, as Seydou continued to watch the house, as well as for activity around the area, Jenny spoke up from the seat in back. "I have an idea, Seydou. Where we stopped much earlier this morning just after we found the highway. The Accra newspaper that was on the table. I kept it by the way." Jenny reached back under a bundle on the back seat and produced the newspaper. "Here it is. While you were checking on the vehicle this morning, I read on the front page a reference to a national contest on TV for finding the smartest high school students in the land. It reads that the contest is open to both boys and girls and people are being encouraged to put forward candidates for the series of quizzes that are to be televised..... I have an idea. About using it to find out if the girls are around. Our objective is finding my daughters, not my husband." Jenny proceeded to explain to Seydou what she had in mind.

"You have a very good imagination, Madame. This could be interesting. I have to think of what I will say." Jenny and Seydou discussed the scenario for Seydou to follow. They would find the village cafe. Seydou would present himself as a recruiter hired by the program to find candidates for the contest. If someone mentioned the Akala daughters, he would ask where they could be found. If he managed to learn that, the basic plan would apply - if the girls showed up and depending on where he was and the presence of other people, he would ask the girls how they could be contacted to follow up. Apart from participating in the contest, would they like to see their mother? He could arrange that. That will of course surprise them. "We would be totally exposed, Madame. The girls could very possibly turn and run and tell their father of the question. We would have to run and it is a long way to getting back out of the country."

Jenny interjected. "Let's see if they are here first, and then if they make contact with you, determine what would be the best step after that. If we know they are here, we can think of a scenario that perhaps has less risk." They went over the details of what Seydou would do and say regarding the contest and the finding out if the girls could be interested. Within twenty minutes, the strategy was set and they returned to the village. Jenny was amazed to learn that Seydou was conversant in the local dialect. Seydou explained to Jenny that in his youth he had been a laborer on the construction of Ghana's major dam and had learned the language of his friends. He returned to Mali at 21 and joined the army. "There is much that I don't know about you, Seydou. I had no idea you spoke Akan."

"Madame, you never asked."

Seydou parked the vehicle behind a cinderblock building that looked to house a car repair shop, accessible from the front. Jenny got on to the back seat, stretched herself out so as not to be seen, while Seydou walked to what appeared to be the village cafe two dusty streets away and out of sight of the Land Rover. He had changed to a clean shirt for what he was about to do.

He entered the cafe and went around with the newspaper article asking if there could be candidates from the village the people would know about. He said he was a recruiter from Accra for the contest. Was it not true the town veterinarian had two daughters who were reputed to be smart? Could they be candidates? Were there others?

One person asked Seydou to remain at the cafe while he went and fetched a grandson. Seydou had little choice but to agree to wait, as long as the wait was not more than twenty minutes, he told the man. The man was back with his grandson within fifteen. Another man insisted on Seydou coming to his home to meet his sister's son after school. Seydou had trouble getting out of that one. He said he would be able to do it only the next day and took directions to the house. In the meantime, he asked the man for the boy's name, year in school and the family's address to be contacted in case he could not make it the next day. In discussions in the cafe, a man finally spoke about the vet's daughters and said they were not around. They were in some Catholic school, 500 kilometers west of there.

Seydou walked to the vehicle. "They are not here, Madame. They are in a Catholic school, one that is apparently 500 kilometers from here. The man who told me that did not know the name of the town or the school."

Jenny slumped in the seat, looked off through the front of the vehicle, then said, "We will go find them, Seydou. I know where to go. Tamale. The archdiocese. They have a list of all the Catholic schools in the north. Five hundred kilometers west of here. That means close to the border. If we can find them, it will be easier to extricate them. And..most important of all, my husband will not be around to stop us. As I remember, the school year in Ghana ends at the end of June. I am disappointed they are not here, but our little plan worked. We at least know where they could be. We have to get out of here."

"Yes, we should. I saw a sign for Tamale."

Jenny and Seydou quickly found the road leading to the capital of the northern region of Ghana that had a sizable Catholic population. They arrived there in early evening, found a modest inn on the outskirts of the city and took two rooms. They were careful to stay away from the larger hotels. Inquisitive police were everywhere in the larger cities in Ghana. A small hotel reduced their chances of being observed. The next morning they found the cathedral with an adjoining administrative office off to the side. Jenny went inside and asked what the Catholic schools for girls were in the general west or northwest region of the country. She informed the nun at the desk that a Ghanaian friend of hers from London had a niece at the school and thought it may be possible for her to learn more about the school and where it was located "Oh, you must be referring to the school at Jirapa. Wonderful school for girls. The best in all of northern Ghana."

"How far is Jirapa from Tamale?" asked Jenny.

"Oh, I suspect about 350 kilometers by car, northwest of here. I have a map somewhere here........Let's see. Jirapa - looking at the scale, I would say 250 kilometers in a straight line, but with the road you must take, it would be 350 kilometers. "

"Sister, are there any other Catholic girls high schools of note in the northwest part of the country?"

"There are schools, Madame, but not high schools that are Catholic for girls only where students actually stay. Is that what you are looking for?"

"Yes. Convent school you would say in the old days. Thank you. I'm sure that's where my friend's niece goes to school. Thank you very much. You have been very helpful." Jenny left and returned to the Land Rover parked in front of the cathedral.

"Jirapa, Seydou. 350 kilometers from here, apparently. Can't be any other place, based on what the nun told me. The only Catholic girls high school in western Ghana that has boarders. Where's the map?"

At 2 PM that afternoon, Seydou and Jenny entered the town of Jirapa and quickly found the school. There was much activity. A group of girls were playing field hockey on a pitch off to the left of the main building, one of three that appeared to comprise the school. A building on the left of the grounds appeared to be a dormitory. Other groups of young women were seated on the steps of the main building. A small group of nuns was strolling along a walkway. Jennie was nervous. She could not hide her excitement. Today could be the day, the moment she sees her daughters for the first time since they were six and three years old.

"I can't take this, Seydou. They have to be here. Please, let them be here."

The plan was for Seydou to enter and enquire. He was to say he was an uncle of the Akala girls and would like to invite them to a family get-together in Wa, the main town south of Jirapa. He would like to speak with them, if he could. Could he use an office for that? Once the girls were in the room, he would ask them if they would like to see their mother. He would ask the question and wait for the answer before telling them their mother was outside.

The plan goes nowhere. The girls are not there anymore. Seydou is informed by the lady at the reception desk that the Akala girls had changed schools the previous September, to a school in Accra. Unfortunately, they did not have the name of the school. It was not given to them at the time.

Seydou left the building and got into the vehicle, knowing full well that the news would be devastating to the lady. "I'm sorry, Madame. They were here but they are no longer here. They changed schools last year, to one in Accra. They don't know which one it is. No name. The nun at the desk could provide no more information than that."

Jenny did not waste a moment. She got out of the vehicle, breezed by Seydou, walked quickly to the entrance to the school, then up the steps and into the building. Seydou could only turn and watch. He could do little to stop her.

"Madame, could I please see the head person of the school?" Jenny asked the lady at the reception desk. "The man who was just here enquired about the Akala girls who were students here. I am their aunt. My sister is their mother. Could I see the principal? Is she here? I would like to speak to her about the girls."

"Well, yes, she is here somewhere in the building. I am sure she would be glad to speak with you. Please wait here. I will fetch her."

Five minutes later, a nun came down the hall and introduced herself as the school headmistress. The name tag on her white uniform read Sister Elizabeth.

"Good morning, Madame. How can I help you?"

"Sister, I am an aunt of Efe and Sisi Akala who were students here in previous years. I am on a visit to the country and thought I would come and try to find them. I live in America and have not seen them in a long time. Their mother has been dead for a number of years and our contacts have become less frequent. I believed they were still students here, but have learned today that is no longer the case, that they were now enrolled in a school in Accra. Just the same, I would like to ask you some questions about them. It has been such a long time. They were little more than babies the last time I saw them."

"Why, of course, Madame. I would be glad to answer your questions about Efe and Sisi. They were good students and very proper young ladies, even through their upbringing was not Catholic. It does not matter so much to us here about that."

"What were they like, Sister? Were they happy? Were they shy or reserved? Were they energetic? Were they inquisitive?"

Jenny continued with her questions before the nun could respond to any more than the first. "Were they good students? How did they, as daughters of a Muslim, do in a Catholic school? Were they out of place?"

The nun listened and observed Jenny while she answered her questions. She knew the woman in front of her could be no one else but the girls' mother.

"You are their mother, aren't you?"

"Yes, I am."

"Only mothers ask those questions the way you asked them."

"My husband and I separated years ago. I have been prevented from seeing my girls ever since. Please don't think badly of me. I have sought desperately to reach them over the years. I was hoping I could see them here. I don't think I will now. I have driven through half of Ghana trying to find them. Accra is big, there are many schools, and it is far. I am afraid this search will have to end. I am not supposed to be here."

"I understand. I will tell no one of this visit. You have my word. Before you leave, however, I believe we have some pictures of your daughters. Follow me." Jenny followed the nun to a room where pictures were tacked to a cork board along a wall. The sister went over, perused the board. "Madame, here is one of your oldest with a couple of friends. There is another one here alone. Now, over here is a picture of the younger one. These pictures are from our end of year picnic last July. You may have the pictures. Please, take them."

Sister Elizabeth spent another twenty minutes answering questions about Efe and Sisi Akala. She could see the anguish of the woman, desperate for news of her estranged children. She did the best she could to describe what she knew of the girls' experience at the school, their personalities and habits, and what she could observe of their characters. "The oldest was very gregarious and sociable - seemingly always at the center of a group. The younger one was more reserved. Both appreciated athletics. Efe in the picture here preferred volleyball, as I remember, whereas Sisi enjoyed playing field hockey." The nun told Jenny what she could remember of the two girls, but the discussion had run its course. "I'm sorry that I have to end this, Madame. I have some things I must attend to this afternoon and it is getting late. I hope I have provided you with some degree of consolation for the fact your daughters are no longer here with us. I do hope you find them. And, again, I will tell no one of your visit."

"Thank you so much, Sister. You have been very kind." Jenny had tears in her eyes as she walked with Sister Elizabeth to the front door of the school.

"Madame, I truly wish the girls were still here. I see your pain." The nun paused a moment, then continued as they reached the door. "I hope you find them. What is your name, by the way?"

"Jennifer. Jennifer Sutton, formerly Akala. Thank you, Sister."

"No one will know of this visit outside of the receptionist and she will never know who you really are. You have my word. God bless."

Jenny and Seydou took to the road west to Burkina Faso, avoided the border checkpoints, and made their way back to Bamako without incident. They knew that going down to Accra would have been futile. The city was huge - close to 2 million people at that time, with dozens of high schools, and 750 kilometers south of Jirapa. Apart from the puzzle of essentially going from high school to high school to see if the Akala girls were enrolled there, the chance that they would escape detection was close to zero. Police routinely stopped motorists on the main roads and asked for their papers. The adventure had to end.

Jenny had pictures of her girls. She couldn't stop looking at them. For long stretches on the road back into Mali, she was silent, looking off in the distance, thinking of what the girls were like, what they did with their time, of what they thought of their mother, of how much she had lost. Somewhere on the road before entering the city of Bobo Dioulasso on the way to Bamako, Jenny declared to Seydou after a long silence, "The battle is not over, Seydou. It has just begun."

At the airport two days later, as Jenny was preparing to exit the vehicle for her flight to Paris and on to New York, she turned to her host, erstwhile bodyguard and escort. "Seydou, you have been wonderful for me. You are a true gentleman and friend. Here is the last amount that I owe you for this."

"I am sorry, Madame. I had hoped you would have your children with you by now. And I cannot take this last payment. We did not succeed. Please, Madame."

"No, Seydou. I insist you take it. You have a large family and have greater use for the money than I. We did not succeed through no fault of yours. I can afford it. Please. *Seydou, j'insiste.* Please. No further argument."

"No further argument, then. But I am sorry you are no closer to your children."

"I am closer to them, Seydou. I have these," holding up the pictures, "and I know where they are. I did not know that before. I had no idea." Jenny paused a moment, then continued before opening the door of the vehicle. "I will have to regroup and find another way. I will stay in touch. I have your address in Nioro. Hopefully, the next time we speak I will have better news to give. Thank you so much."

"Au revoir, Madame. Let me know how it all goes. *Je suis à votre service pour toujours."*

PART THREE

21

Six months later, November 1990

"Tim, I found someone in Accra to help me and she has found where my daughters go to school." Jenny was bubbling with excitement on the phone. "Someone I worked with at the travel agency years ago. Happened quickly."

"Great, Jenny. How did it come about? From what you have told me, all your avenues were pretty much dried up."

"I found, in some old papers, the number of a friend, a certain Judith who I used to work with. It was where she used to live when I was in Ghana. I asked for Judith Osuma, and right away I was given the number where she now lived. I called and lo and behold, Judith answered. We spoke for close to an hour. This was a week ago. Well, this morning she called me and said there was an Efe Akala in 11th grade at Saint Francis High School in Accra and a Sisi Akala in 9th grade. I know where they are!"

"How did she get the information? She just asked?" asked Tim, knowing the difficulties getting information from institutions anywhere, let alone Africa.

"It was the fourth Catholic high school she called. There are over twenty of those in Accra. She said she was a friend of the sister of the Akala girls' deceased mother and was trying to locate the girls so that the aunt who lived in America could write to them, care of the school. The secretary of the school said they had an Efe Akala, and a Sisi Akala. She told Judith she could send a letter care of the school..... I know where they are now! I can write to them!"

"Happy for you, Jenny. This may finally get you somewhere. Let me know what I can do to help."

"I will have to be careful with the letters. Never know who could intercept them. I am always thinking of Korafa, of what he could still do. He is back in Ghana, by the way, and I am sure he would love to find a way to punish me. Punish would be the kind word, actually."

"OK. By the way, I saw Jay on Monday evening. He was in Boston covering a story and we had dinner. He would like to see you. I gave him your number."

"No problem. I want to hear from him what happened to that story he was supposed to write. Have to run, Tim. Need to write that letter to my little girls who are no longer little. The picture I have from their previous school appears they are almost as tall as I am."

Two days later.

"Tim, I just got a phone call from Judith in Accra. She was crying. Said she was visited by a man who told her not to enquire anymore about the Akala girls. He made her admit she had called me with the information on their whereabouts. Judith said the man twisted her arm, threatened to do more. She was calling from a friend's house, and was terrified." Jenny paused a moment, then continued. "The grandmother. I'm sure of it.

Threatening anyone and everyone communicating with me. I can't believe this."

Jenny had written a letter to her daughters. She had mailed it the day before, care of Air Mail Express, before receiving the phone call. She was told the letter would arrive within four days.

Two weeks later, Jenny called the number of St. Francis High School in Accra. She asked if she could speak with the principal. She was put through to a Sister Angela. The conversation did not last long. "Madame, I am not at liberty to speak with you about the young women who you claim are your daughters. I have been requested by the girls' family to not speak with you or anyone who claims to be enquiring on your behalf. I am sorry. I must obey the request of the family."

Jenny was aghast. "Sister, the girls are my daughters. I have been prevented from seeing or speaking with them for over ten years. You do not realize the anguish this has caused me. I beg you to let me explain and hopefully relent, despite what the girls' father says. I sent them a letter two weeks ago, care of the school. Was it received?"

"The order is not from their father, Madame. It is from their grandmother. But it is no less an order that I must respect. I am told you abandoned the children and have had no contact with them for ten years. I gave their grandmother your letter. I was bound to respecting the family's wishes."

"I did not abandon them, Sister. They were taken from me. I have written them faithfully every month over those ten years, but I surmise all those letters like the one I sent two weeks ago were intercepted. My daughters have been most probably told I abandoned them, that I don't care, but that is furthest from the truth. Please, Sister, I implore you. Let me speak with them. Put me through to them. I am their mother. I beg you."

"I am sorry, Madame. I cannot do that. I am truly sorry. I would like to believe you, but I must end this call. The Akala family is very important here. My hands are tied. Goodbye."

Threatening Judith. Scaring her half to death. Ordering the nuns to cut me off. They know all about what I have been doing..... Sahr, the man I loved. And the Momma. The manipulator. The controlling witch of the Akala clan. Jenny left the office, found the elevator down to the street, walked the three blocks up to Central Park, found a bench, sat down, watched the pigeons mill about on the path and realized she had no idea what to do next. She was at a loss. The tears came.

Yendi, three weeks before......

The man had arrived at the clinic with a sick billy goat, the pride of the small herd he had that supplemented his family's trucking business.

"Doctor Akala, I saw your American wife a few weeks ago. Your first wife. Bless Allah. She is back. Good for you. She was a beautiful woman and still is. I am sure you are happy."

Sahr Akala was dumbfounded. "You what? You saw my wife? Where? When was this?"

"At the truck stop and restaurant before Yendi on the road from Paga. I am sure it was her. Tall, dark haired, although her head was covered. She was in a Land Rover. I am sure it was her.

Why are you so surprised?" replied the part-time herder and trucker.

"It cannot be my wife. My wife has been gone for over ten years. She left the family. It had to be someone else." Sahr Akala had difficulty concealing his unease. Could it be? Is she around? What is going on? Does she know where the girls are? An inner anticipation was working inside him. An excitement he could not repress.

"Well, Doctor, I was pretty sure it was your wife. The driver was African, although I had never seen him before. I could be mistaken. I probably was. I am sorry for bringing it up."

That evening Sahr mentioned the discussion with the herder to his mother. The next day Madame Akala made enquiries in the town. No one could recall seeing a tall white woman anywhere in the village a few weeks before. Sahr went out to the truck stop a few kilometers from Yendi and asked the owner if he had seen a tall dark haired Caucasian woman in a vehicle stop there a few weeks before. The owner said he had seen probably a dozen white women coming through and stopping at his place for a cola and petrol in the past few weeks. "The road is well travelled, sir, and not just by Africans." He went back to work on the car he was servicing before Sahr could ask another question.

In the meantime, Sahr's mother surmised that Jenny could very well have discovered where the girls were. She did not doubt that the woman the herder saw was her son's first wife. Once you saw Jenny Sutton Akala, you remembered her. She called St. Francis High School, spoke to the principal, and asked her to refrain from allowing anyone from the outside making contact with the Akala girls. The principal had asked Madame

Akala who those persons could be and received the reply that it could be a woman who claimed to be the girls' mother. She said the girls' mother had disappeared ten years before, abandoning her family. It would be highly unlikely that person would be the girls' mother.

She also placed a call to the man who had been Colonel Korafa's deputy, in the days when Korafa was still in the good graces of the family. "Go to the school. Find out however you can if anyone has been trying to reach the Akala girls or enquiring about them. Their names are Efe and Sisi. Report back to me."

"Yes, Madame."

Accra, April 1991

Wilson Kuma and Mustafa Korafa had not seen each other for a year, a few weeks after the latter had arrived back in Ghana from America. Kuma had been one of Korafa's trusted deputies in the secret service before Korafa's banishment to the north. It was Kuma who had monitored the movements and communications of the American woman in the early 1980's, as well as of the people who were in contact with her just before her leaving the country. While his boss Korafa was still in the good graces of the Akala family, Kuma had met the veterinarian's mother. In the years following Korafa's demise, he had been called upon by the government to provide services to the Akala matriarch upon request. It was he who Madame Akala contacted to deal with the young woman in Accra who was enquiring about her granddaughters at their school.

"The American woman who you asked me to follow years ago has resurfaced, Mustafa. It appears she has been trying to re-establish contact with her children."

Kuma proceeded to tell Korafa of Jennifer's inquiries and the reactions of the Akala family, especially those of the grandmother. The former agent went on and described how he had contacted Jennifer's friend in Accra and warned her off. He told Korafa that he was quite sure the woman would cease acting on the American woman's behalf. Korafa looked at his erstwhile deputy of years before. So, she is messing around here now, he thought. After a moment of silence, he said, "You know it was the Akalas who put me in the gulag up north. I lost my job as Director because of them. They also had me sacked from the job in Washington. I have nothing but contempt for them, Kuma, but just the same, I thank you for this."

22

A few days later in New York

"Jenny, this is Jay Peterson. Tim Hurley gave me your contact information. I would like to see you. Could we have dinner sometime? It will be on me."

"Jay Peterson. Yes. I would love to see you. It has been a long time since that evening in Accra. Much has happened since then. I don't know what Tim has told you. We speak every once in awhile. It is certainly very short notice, but how about this evening? I have nothing planned."

"Sure. This evening is fine. I have nothing planned either. Just as well. Tell me where it would be convenient for you."

"I work in Midtown, Jay. I can meet you at the Greek restaurant, I don't remember the name but it is fabulous, a couple doors down from the Harvard Club on 44th at 7:30. You can't miss it, it is towards 5th Avenue. I have the name somewhere and will make the reservation. I'll go there from the office. Would that be all right?"

"Right on, Jenny. Look forward to it. I will tell you about the article I wrote that never appeared. I owe it to you. See you later."

Jenny and Jay shared just about everything that had happened in their lives, starting from where they left each other that night at the out-of-the-way restaurant outside of Accra. Jay told Jenny what had happened with the story - the write-up, the difficulties with getting anyone to talk to him in Accra, his anger and disgust with it being turned down, with it all leading to his leaving NewsWorld.

As they finished dinner, Jay told Jenny of other elements of the story. "You probably did not know this at the time, Jenny, but I had discovered there was a big competition going on in Accra between the United States and China over the award of mineral rights in the country. An American company had given a big bribe to the Minister of the Interior and the U.S. Government had to cover it up. Moreover, there was a reluctance on the part of the U.S. Government to do anything that would upset the local government. There was a lot at stake in those years. Nobody at the Embassy would talk to me. It could very well have had a lot to do with the Embassy's indifference to your situation."

What Jay told Jenny about the Minister of the Interior caused a light to go on. "Jay, you know, I believe I told you when we met, the Minister of the Interior at the time was the cousin of my mother-in-law. The cunning old witch who has been behind all my troubles." Jenny thought for a moment before continuing. "The bribe, the soft approach with Ghana, there it is. The rat of a consul-general, Keyes was his name, would have known of my family connection to the Interior Minister. He would not have intervened even if I had slept with him. Hmm. No wonder. There was no way he was going to help me. He needed to avoid causing problems with the family and by extension the Minister doling out mineral rights. I have an 'f' word in mind, but I won't say it."

"I'm afraid you're right, Jenny. I had surmised that, and put it in the article. But I couldn't get anyone to substantiate anything. My editor would not let it go. I was pissed, believe me."

Jay proceeded to tell Jenny about Tim Hurley and a friend of his, Brian Maxwell, who had run into Margaret Bishop in London. "Tim thinks you should get back in touch with Margaret. She still has some contacts in Ghana that could be of assistance. I don't know what those could be, but Tim suggested that, if I managed to see you, tell you that you should get in touch with her."

"I know Brian. He was the first of all of you I told of my predicament. We lost touch after that. Do you have Margaret's contact information? I'd love to speak to her. We had a good friendship back in Ghana. Her aid organization had agreed to finance the operations of a girls school I was setting up in Yendi. It all got put off with my banishment."

"Yes, you told me about that. Anyway, Tim will have Margaret's info, where you can reach her."

The next day, the lady with the distinctive British public school accent answered the phone. "Hello."

"How's Buckeye, Margaret?"

"Why, Jenny. Jenny. Jenny. How are you? So good to hear your voice. To what do I owe the privilege of this call, my dear?"

"I ran into a friend last evening, who spoke about Brian Maxwell of Paris running into a Margaret Bishop who knew me. It provided a good excuse for me to call you. How are you?"

"I am fine. Semi-retired, my dear, but enjoying it. And your Buckeye has been a dear friend to me all these years. This is quite a surprise. You will have to tell me about the situation with your children. Did you get resolution?"

"No, I haven't, Margaret. It has been a long road and it is still a tortuous one, a never-ending saga. I am despairing of seeing them, I must admit. My government has not helped me at all. It is a very difficult situation. I don't know if I will ever get back with them."

Jenny needed to change the subject. "What are you doing, Margaret? Semi-retired. What does the semi part of it mean?"

"Working part-time with an international NGO that helps finance and develop centers for orphaned girls and destitute women in third world countries. Not all that far from what I was doing in Ghana, actually. I can still collect my government pension."

"Tell me about it. I have a latent interest in the subject. You will remember the school we came close to setting up in Ghana."

"Of course. The focus is generally the same in the countries where the NGO operates. We discover a school serving young girls from the poorer classes, or rather they discover us, and we find ways to help the ones who qualify for aid and are the greatest in need. What would interest you, Jenny?"

"I get to London from time to time with my job. Like I said, I have a latent interest in the subject of schooling and hostels for poor girls. My mother was an orphan and I always told her I would someday help orphaned girls one way or the other. This is what you do, Margaret. There may be some way I could help. I will contact you soon. I would love to see Buckeye, for one, and give you a big hug once again."

"Jenny, love to have you here in London. Let me know when you come. I don't believe I will be in New York any time soon. We'll probably end up reconnecting here. All the best and a big hug as well."

Two weeks later..

Jenny was in Washington. She was attending a philanthropic awards dinner at the Kennedy Center for the Performing Arts, representing McGuire Media. Sitting next to her was Senator Bruce Dauber, Democratic Senator from Minnesota and a member of the Senate Foreign Relations Committee.

After some discussion of McGuire Media and its activities in promoting equal opportunities for visible minorities, Senator Dauber leaned over to Jenny. "Ms. Sutton, you have a family, I suppose. How are they doing?" It was an innocent enough question, meant to ease conversation away from the subject of the evening, which they had amply covered to that time.

"Senator, I do have a family, but I have been estranged from it for twelve years. I wish I could tell you my children are doing well, but I have to tell that I don't know if that's the case. They are far away in Africa. It has been difficult for me." Jenny knew full well from the beginning of the evening that the encounter with the Senator she was placed next to could lead to a discussion of her situation and she was prepared for it. She didn't even have to bring it up. He did.

"My God, what is this about? Africa you say. What is the situation with your family? Estranged. Does that mean forcibly? Is it something that the United States government should be aware of? Lots of questions here. What do you want to tell me about this?"

Jenny looked intently at the Senator and decided that his expression of interest was genuine. She would tell him everything that was important. Dessert was coming and the dinner would be breaking up soon. She had nothing to lose. She finished her story. "Frankly, Senator, the government has betrayed me. I do not have good words to say about its support."

"What did they not do, in your view?" asked the Senator.

"They did nothing, absolutely nothing to intervene with the Government of Ghana on my behalf. My two little girls were born in the United States. They were and still are American citizens. There are the laws of Ghana about paternal prerogative, but there are also American laws that apply to its native-born citizens. Not only was there no intervention on my behalf by the State Department, there was not even any intent by consular officials in Accra to intervene. I can tell you more, if you wish. It's not nice."

"This is not the place to get into any further detail about this, Ms. Sutton. Jenny is your name, right?" Jenny nodded, and the Senator continued, "I want you call me in the next few days to set up a meeting in my office. Here is my card. My assistant's name is Anne. I will tell her to expect a call from you. I want to know more about your situation and what the US government did or did not do and has or has not done on your behalf since your time in Africa. I am a member of the Foreign Relations

Committee and have a particular interest in how our State Department looks after our citizens abroad."

"I will do that, Senator. I will call Anne tomorrow. I work in Manhattan and coming to Washington is not a problem."

"You will tell me when we meet what you would like to keep personal. I have no interest in doing anything to make things worse for you, but I will want to know as much as you are willing to tell me about your dealings with the government. Through all this we will see to what extent I can be of assistance to get your children back."

"Thank you, Sir." The dinner broke up soon after and the Senator was surrounded by people wishing to say hello, shake his hand, have a picture taken with him. It was a typical scene for political Washington. But Jenny had gotten his attention and went back to her hotel feeling good about the encounter.

At the meeting in the Senator's office, the discussion did not take long. Jenny covered everything relevant within twenty minutes. The Senator had an aide with him who took notes. She spoke of the actions of the consul-general, the insinuation he would help in exchange for favors, the unsuccessful enquiries when back in New York. She told of the non-existence of her and the girls' files in Accra, the intimidation from the Ghanaian Embassy, the desperation of her trip to Ghana through the bush from Mali, the exchanges with the school in Accra and the threats to the lady there who tried to help her. The senator told her he would look into the matter.

Two weeks later, Jenny received a call from him. "Jenny, the State Department has indicated to me that they are willing to do all they can to get you access to your children. You will have to come to Washington and meet an official at State. This is her name. She is an assistant undersecretary. Here is her direct number. She will meet with you. We will start with that. You will have to repeat everything you told me and probably more. But she assured me she would do all she could. It helps to be on the Senate committee that looks after their operations."

"Senator, I appreciate this very much. What can I do to thank you?"

"Let me know what happens. It's a start. We will see what we can do. All the best, Ms. Sutton."

Jenny met Susan Riley and told her everything. Three months later in late August, Jenny was invited back to Washington for what the assistant undersecretary called a debrief. She was told that the file had been reopened and that they had found anomalies in the way it had been treated in Accra and afterwards back in Washington. Miss Riley told Jenny at the beginning of the meeting that everything she would be told that day would have to remain within the four walls of the room. Only with that proviso could she share the contents of the file with Jenny. Jenny gave her consent.

Jenny was then told that Richard Keyes had left the employ of the government. In their check of the files, officials had found evidence that information on Jennifer Sutton Akala and her children had been tampered with, apparently deliberately misplaced to avoid detection through the regular annual audits of consular files. It was clear that the consul-general had done nothing in Accra to pressure the government there to provide Jenny with access to her children, despite the fact they were American citizens. On two occasions in memos to Washington that were found, it was noted that her request for the Government to intervene on her behalf with the Government of Ghana should be treated with reserve as she was the one who had abandoned her children and therefore had forfeited her right of access. The notes implied that her situation was all her fault. The assistant undersecretary told Jenny that the consul-general implied they had found that she was promiscuous and could not be counted on for the truth. Very unflattering, if not damaging allegations, said the official to Jenny, but then stated that the former consul-general had since been discredited and had left the foreign service under a cloud. Much of what he had written about affairs in Ghana in notes to Washington during his time there had been discovered to be suspect, if not untrue in some cases. "The information I have just given you stays with us, Mrs. Sutton. It has been discredited and will go no further. You can be assured of that." She said she did not know where Richard Keyes was. She then went on to say that she had some good news for her. "The Africa desk at State is willing to intercede on your behalf in Accra. The ambassador to Ghana has been apprised of the file. I believe things will begin to happen, Ms. Sutton. Senator Dauber has spoken with him. It may take some time, but things will move."

A month later, Susan Riley called her. "Things are happening, Jenny. Our ambassador there apparently has had a long acquaintance with the new Ghanaian Minister of Foreign Affairs They met years ago when they both were posted in London. They spoke about your case a few days ago. By the way, since the election of the new administration, there has been a definite improvement in relations with Ghana as with other governments in Africa, with the two governments working more closely than they have in the past. In any case, the Ambassador called me this morning to say that the Minister told him the government would not object to US Embassy officials speaking with the school where the girls were. Given that the girls were

American citizens, they could be asked by the U.S. Embassy official who would go to the school if they would like to communicate with their mother."

"The understanding was that the school would be contacted by an official of the foreign affairs department of Ghana and told to cooperate with the American request. However, if the girls did not want to meet the official or meet you in the end there was nothing else anyone could do. That was the understanding between the Ambassador and the Minister. There was no question of having anyone coerce your daughters into something against their wishes."

"Would that be something acceptable to you, Jenny? Your daughters will be told you are alive, that you have tried to reach them to no avail, that they could meet with you if they wished. What do you think? We are willing to orchestrate that."

Jenny took no time to respond. "That would be great. It would be wonderful. When can it be done?"

"As soon as next week. Someone from the Embassy will call the school and arrange for a meeting with your daughters. Are we on?"

"We're on," said Jenny.

The word came back three weeks later that the girls told the American official that their mother had abandoned them, that they had received no news from her, contrary to what the Embassy person was saying, that they had been very upset about that since they were little. The American official who met the girls said that the youngest one did not have any recollection of her mother. He did not detect any evidence that the girls had been coerced to refuse the encounter with their mother, but did say that they were agitated and not comfortable at all with the prospect of that sort of meeting. There was nothing more the Embassy could do. They were sorry to have to report this.

Susan Riley was practically despondent at the other end of the line when telling Jenny the news. Jenny was devastated. She began to see the whole exercise as futile. The Akalas were still winning and I can't change anything. The girls don't even want to see me. She was despairing of ever seeing them again.

23

A few days after the news had come in from Accra, Jenny decided to take a week off and go see her niece and nephew in San Diego. Change the scenery. Do some family. She had her staff reschedule whatever meetings had been planned. Her boss had learned what had happened. "Get out of here, Jenny. Take a break. There's nothing here we can't do."

She rented a house outside of La Jolla up the coast, walked to the beach every day, and had Karen, the twenty-year old daughter of her long-lost brother, with her for part of the time she was there. Her nephew Sean, a senior in college, came by the hacienda on two of the evenings. Jenny took them to dinner the days they were around. Sean was graduating in marketing in the spring and told Jenny he was looking for guidance on jobs. Jenny would end up putting him in touch with recruiters at a number of her clients when she got back to New York. Jenny and the children of her brother they never knew managed to have a good time in the hours they spent together. Sean and Karen both had always been curious to learn about what had happened to their cousins who left for Africa so long ago. They had never met them. Jenny had told them over the years in general terms what had happened. She related to them her most recent efforts. "I'm afraid I don't know what to do anymore. I may never see them again." Despite the relaxing time she spent those nine days, the pain would not go away. Jenny was back in New York with much the same melancholy she had the day she left for California.

The assistant was at the door to her office. "Jenny, Paul Russo is on the line. Do you want to talk to him?"

"Put him through."

"Paul, how are you doing?

"Hey, Jen, I'm fine. I hope you are as well, but I suspect not. I found out about the turn-down from your daughters. I'm sorry."

"How did you know, Paul? I didn't exactly broadcast it."

"There are people in your company for whom you are a dear person and with whom I am friends. New York is New York. Things get around. Don't be mad at anyone for that." Paul hesitated a moment, then continued. "I've got something for you. A change of pace. How about a weekend in Stowe? Some skiing, some good food. It will be on me. I won't bother you. We'll have separate rooms. How about it?"

"Paul Russo, I think I will accept. From the desert to snow banks with Paul Russo. Yes. I can do that. What weekend do you have in mind?"

He had reserved two rooms at one of the nicer lodges and a stone's throw from Stowe Mountain. It was two weeks before Christmas in December 1991. He and Jenny took a Friday afternoon flight from Newark to Burlington, rented a car and arrived in time for dinner. Jenny spent the dinner telling Paul about her clandestine trip into Ghana the year before and the events that had followed. She began to relax and at the end of the evening, he escorted her to her room, gave her a peck on the

146

cheek and said he would knock on her door at 8 for breakfast, get sized up for skis, bindings and all that and then hit the slopes.

They spent the following day skiing in the morning, having a quick lunch at the lodge on the crest of the mountain, then some more skiing, with the rest of the afternoon at the spa with alternating dips in a cold stream and a Turkish steam bath. Dinner with a bottle of wine followed the spa and a double round of martinis. Jenny had managed to relax and appreciated Paul's company. Talk of her children and her saga to regain them was a long way from the discussion. The talk went from racing cars in crazy overland races - Dakar was but one of the races Paul participated in - to his job in the financial sector to his own family and its roots in Italy and Brooklyn.

After a pause in the discussion, with their wine glasses nearly empty and their plates taken away, Paul looked at Jenny and blurted out, "Jenny, we were cool the whole time of the race, from start to finish. It was the deal. But I'm hooked on you, my dear. Can we give it a try?" He paused a moment, then continued, "You must know, though, that you don't have to say yes."

Jenny looked back, and then said mischievously with a smile on her face. "I've been thinking about something like that as well, as we sit here. I admit it. Let's give it a try. Pay the bill. Let's go to my room."

It would be the first of many weekends with Paul. It was also the first of many other liaisons. Over the following six months, Jenny threw her reserve out the window. She accepted requests for dates that she had always turned down before. She was 40, in great shape, and an extremely attractive woman. She had money, position, and influence in corporate America. Her clients ran from Coca-Cola to Procter & Gamble to Estee Lauder.

Up to that time, she had shied away from any intimate relationships with men. A one-night stand with a producer in LA four years before. Not enjoyable. That was it for sex since her last night in bed with Sahr in Yendi thirteen years before. She had lots of offers. It was New York. The advertising business was conducive to it. She had turned them all away.

But with the despair, the anger, the sorrow, the self-pity, she ran loose as they say in New York. She had begun to drink. Martinis before dinner, wine at dinner, sex afterwards. She was in distress. Her work began to suffer. Her colleagues noticed. Paul despaired at Jenny's behavior. He had wanted to have a relationship with her, but not like this, not in sharing her with other men. He went to her apartment one evening and gave her hell.

"What are you doing? You're making yourself into a mess. This is not what I had in mind when we started this, Jenny."

Jenny broke down and cried, sobbing in Paul's arms half the night. In the middle of it, she got up, took a bottle of Vodka from the freezer and drowned her sorrow with half of it. Paul sat there and watched, then after an hour or two, got up and left. The relationship was over. It was not the relationship he wanted.

24

New York, June 1992

"Hello, Jenny. How nice to see you again." Jenny recoiled as she moved through the crowd at the reception on the ground floor of the mid-town office tower.

"Stay away from me. Leave me alone."

The balding, middle-aged man showed no emotion as Jenny hissed her anger at his reappearance into her life.

"I didn't know you were in New York. A long ways from Accra, is it not?" Richard Keyes paused a moment. The former career diplomat and onetime deputy head of mission of the United States Embassy in Ghana, was now Chief of Protocol of the City of New York. He continued in his address to the lady in the midst of the large crowd. "It seems you work here, Jenny. You look to be in charge. Good show. What happened to your kids?"

"My kids are none of your business any more. Goodbye, Mr. Keyes," as she moved away into the crowd that had gathered for the charity event she had helped organize.

The man did not follow Jenny but a few days later began a series of phone calls to her office. Twice a week, like clockwork for a month. She hung up when he called, then began to have her assistant screen all her calls which she had never done before. Clients appreciated that Jenny would always take her own calls. Before hanging up at the fourth or fifth one from Richard Keyes, she said forcefully, "Leave me alone. I don't want to see you. I don't walk to talk to you. I want nothing to do with you. Is that clear?"

"Jenny, I just want to talk to you. I am sorry about what happened in Ghana. It has been a long time. I want to make it up to you." Jenny hung up before he could say anything else.

At what she believed to be the eighth or ninth call from Keyes, Jenny decided to register a complaint with the police. She phoned the local precinct. She wanted to know what they could do to get harassment to stop. A day later, she received a call from a police lieutenant who told her there was a Richard Keyes who was the City's Chief of Protocol. He had a photo and wanted her to tell him if he could come by and have her say if this was the man who was harassing her. The lieutenant showed up a half-hour later. "Is this him?"

"Yes, Lieutenant, and I don't care what he does for the city. It has to stop."

"Ms. Sutton, I understand, but I have to tell you something. Mr. Keyes' brother is the Police Commissioner of New York. My boss in the end. And like I said, Mr. Keyes in the picture here is the Chief of Protocol of the City of New York. It doesn't mean that the man has immunity, but this will have to be handled with some discretion. It will be a delicate matter. Please let me know if the calls continue." The lieutenant left. Jenny put her head in her hands. I can't believe this. Chief of protocol for the city and his brother is the Police Commissioner. Incredible. How do I deserve this?

After a week of peace, Jenny's assistant came to the door one Tuesday morning and announced that "the man is calling again. I told him you were not here."

Jay had not seen Jenny for over a year. His political reporting for NewsMag had taken him across the country, reporting on the state of the nation in advance of the 1992 elections. "Jenny, it's Jay. Long time no see. Taking a chance here. Are you free for lunch today?"

"Yes, good idea. I'll make myself free. Where do we meet?"

"The bar at the Regis. 12:15?"

"Good. See you then."

She's just as attractive as ever, he thought as he saw Jenny enter the King Cole Bar of the hotel. And what a resilient lady.

"Jenny, you look great, as always. Good to see you."

"Thank you, Jay. I may seem to look great, but I am not in the best of shape, I must say. I'll fill you in a bit, if you want."

"You have quite a story. I have always been intrigued with it. Tell me what has happened, but not before we have a glass of wine."

The waiter arrived with the wine. Jenny opened up and told Jay all about her recent life.

They finished their lunch. "Jay, I have to be back at the office. Appreciated this. Hope I didn't bore you with it. Good to have someone to talk to, though."

"Jenny, let's keep in touch. I mean in the days, weeks to come. I hope you can consider me a friend. I have followed all of this from afar for years. I am there to help. I mean it. I am still a writer. There is the power of the pen. Let me know what you decide to do."

"Thank you, Jay. I will let you know. All the best," said Jenny as she rose from the table.

At 8 AM the next morning, 1 PM in London, she placed a call to Margaret Bishop.

"Margaret, this is Jenny Sutton. Calling you from New York. How are you?"

"I am fine, my dear. How are you?"

"Margaret, I want to leave New York. Get away for awhile. I have had a setback in my efforts to reunite with my children. It has become a hell for me. I can't continue to stay here. You mentioned the last time we spoke you were working with a network of orphanage schools in Asia. I have thought about that. Do you think there would be a place that would take me on? I don't need to be paid a lot, if at all. Would that be possible?"

Her reply was quick. "That would be entirely possible, Jenny. I have an idea. We can talk about it. But, what happened? What's the setback?"

Jenny told her what had happened with the Embassy and the girls' school in Accra.

"My God, when will this be over for you?"

"I don't know, but I need to get away. What is your idea?"

"There is a school in rural India supported by aid from the U.K. Government that could use a helping hand, to manage the foreign aid and related relationships that they have been obliged to develop. They could use assistance in general management as well, I am told. It is out of the way in a remote part of one of India's many provinces. I could contact them through the High Commission in Delhi and see if they would be interested in having you. Do you want me to pursue this? I will have to have a resume for you if you do."

"Yes, Margaret, please do. I will fax you a resume. What's the fax number at your office?"

"I will call you as soon as I hear back, my dear. Keep the faith."

A month later.....

"Jenny, Margaret here. I spoke to the aid officer at the High Commission today. He had managed to reach the school in Madya Pradesh I told you about. They are interested in having you. It is not easy to reach them. Madya Pradesh province is one of the poorest of India, largely cut off from much of the recent development in the country. One of the administrators was in Delhi by chance a few days ago, was shown your resume and told the official at the Commission that you would be welcome. They would feed and house you, but would have little extra to pay you with. They were told you did not expect a salary. With that, they quickly agreed to receive you. They apprently had good experience in the past with American volunteers."

"This is great, Margaret," replied Jenny. "I need to take a day or two to reflect on it, but I think I'm going to do it. What do I need to do now?"

Margaret told Jenny what she needed to do. "You will be free to go there any time. Just have to let them know when you plan to arrive." She suggested that Jenny stop in London on the way to India to meet with the aid organization that funds the school.

Jenny put the wheels in motion for an indefinite leave of absence from McGuire Media and New York. She informed her boss. "Support you 100%, Jenny. We all know what you have been through with your children. I don't relish not having you with us, but we will make do. Take your time. You will always be welcome back. I hope you know that," he said. She put her condo up for rent and within days had found a suitable couple to rent it for a year. If Jenny came back from India in the meantime and wanted the apartment back, the couple would have three months to find something else and would not have to pay the final two months. An acceptable compromise. Jenny was not sure if she would manage to stay in India for more than a few months, but she couldn't have her condo vacant all that time. She had her furniture, clothes and other belongings put into storage, and made plans to leave New York. Her last weekend was spent at her sister's home in Maryland, with Molly's family and the children of her sister Margie that she had been so close to. The thirteen years since Jenny's return from Africa had seen her become the doting aunt for of all her siblings' children.

A few days before she left for India, she had a long lunch in Manhattan with Tim Hurley and Jay Peterson, both of whom wanted to give Jenny a warm send-off before her journey.

After hearing what she could tell them of the school she would be going to, Tim said, "I don't think I ever told you about this, but I had an experience a few years ago in Thailand that has some relevance to what you will be dealing with in India, as I understand it. Sordid state of affairs for young women - all women as a matter of fact - as well as for children."

"What was it about?" asked Jenny. "How does something you experienced in Thailand relate to my going to India?"

Tim related to Jenny and Jay his experience with the Lao girl in Thailand. "It had a happy ending. My bringing her to the embassies led her to being admitted into Canada. She got to Montreal, found a guy who she has since married and seems to be happy. Sends me a note with a picture of her and her husband and child now every year. She got out. Seems like the place she was detained in could have used some people like you, Jenny."

"Hmm. Where was it, Tim? Do you remember the name of the place?" asked Jenny. "Do you know if it still exists?"

"No, I don't. It was near a town called Nong Khai close to the border with Laos. I don't remember the name but I could easily find out if I looked at a map. I went there. Got close enough to see it was not nice. Maybe still exists. I don't know," said Tim.

"Interesting. In any case, I'm going to India, not Thailand, and I'm glad to leave New York. Not sure about a long life in an Indian village. Re-connecting with my children is another story. I wish I had some hope, but that is rapidly running out. Need to move on." Jenny took a deep breath, paused, looked at Tim and Jay across the table, then continued. "I've talked about me the whole time. What's happening with you guys?"

After the farewell that day in New York, Jay Peterson decided to do some digging on Ghana. Need to help her. This story is not over. They can't get away with this. Kids duped and lied to. Nuts.

"Amy, I need you to do something for me." Jay had reached his old colleague, from NewsWorld Africa days, Amy Leach. She had left NewsWorld a few years before and became freelance after marrying a French businessman in Dakar.

"It's about the lady in Accra I wrote the story about years ago." Jay had told Amy Jenny's story when he informed her years before of why he had left NewsWorld. "I am trying to think of some way to help the lady get her kids back. Her in-laws control access to them, and that will always be difficult, but an intelligence guy who pursued her over there is a threat to her life. Getting the kids is one thing. He and what he can do to her is another. I believe that if I organize or attempt to do anything above board to reunite Jenny with her kids, that guy has the motivation as well as the resources to cause trouble. His pursuit of her has cost him his job, his power, and most probably his income. This story, this very real story, has been on my mind for years. The nightmare for her has gone on for a long time. She is so in despair she is going off to some distant place in the depths of India to lose herself."

"What do you want me to do?"

"Can I get you to do some digging?"

"Jay, you always helped me back in the old days. I know you well enough to know you won't be asking me to do something I can't deliver on. Give me the details I can work with. What do you want to know?" she asked. "I have to go to Accra soon about something else, in any case."

Two weeks later Amy called Jay in New York.

"Jay, here are some elements to this. As to the Minister of the Interior, Akwasi Agya, the cousin of the matriarch of the Akala family and grandmother of the daughters, the Ghanaian government picked up on some rumors. They found out that he had taken bribes from American, French and Chinese companies for years without letting the President or colleagues know about it. The money had apparently been used to expand the wealth of the extended Akala family in the north, allowing them to buy local elections and maintain their power. The President became incensed at this when he learned of it, and had come close to sacking the Minister. Only a multi-million dollar contribution to the President's own re-election campaign had stayed the decision. It was a scandal being kept under wraps."

"Interesting," said Jay. "But it sounds like the Akala family interests are in some jeopardy. What about Korafa, the intelligence guy?"

"He's disappeared. Was sent back from a posting in Washington like you said and has become invisible. My sources in the military and diplomatic service tell me they don't know where he is or what he is doing. All they know is that he was discharged from the military. Orders from the top. Nobody has seen or heard from him."

"Amy, thanks for this. I'm not sure what I am going to do with it. This story is definitely not over, though. This adds to it."

"Anything else you want me to do? Are there other angles you need to check out from here?"

"Don't know yet. Need to think about it. I'll let you know."

25

Mustafa Korafa knew all about the troubles Akwasi Agya and the Akala family had with the President and his entourage. He had made a point of tracking the actions of the Minister and the family since returning to Ghana, through his own resources and those of others. Over the years, he also had maintained ties with Russian intelligence. He was now living quietly in a town not far from Tamale in the north of the country, away from the eyes of government, helping a friend run a car repair shop. But he essentially earned his living by reporting to the Russians on what he knew about African security services and matters relative to their interests in Ghana. He knew a lot about people involved in intelligence across the continent. The Russians believed he could be useful and paid him a retainer nobody knew about. They told him of many things they learned on their own. From time to time, they would share information of their eavesdropping on the President and Minister Agya, knowing that he had it in for the Agya and Akala families, and for the President who had sacked him two years before. They knew all about the bribes from American, French and Chinese companies to the Minister over the years. What interested the Russians in all this was embarrassing the Americans and Chinese in the chase for influence as well as in the control of mineral trade in the world.

"Sahr, I must speak with you. Can we meet in Accra next week? Specifically Tuesday, if you could. I can't tell you what this is about now, but I encourage you to come and hear what I have to say. We would meet at a place outside the city. Can you make it?" The caller was Sahr's old friend from school, Manu Nrumah, who had been Ambassador to the United States at one time and was now the Undersecretary for External Affairs, the most powerful civil servant in the diplomatic service of Ghana. He was the man who had Mustafa Korafa sent back from Washington, which led to his being expelled from the military and from all further government service.

"Yes, if you say so, Manu." Sahr knew that this was important. His old friend would not be speaking to him in this way about a trivial matter. "Where do you propose we do this?"

Sahr met him at the out-of-the-way bar in the Accra suburb the following Tuesday.

"My old friend, what I am going to tell you must go no further. This is about your family. I am doing this is as a favor. Can I have your word that this meeting has never happened? I have not had this listed anywhere in my agenda. Nobody on my end knows we are meeting. Have you told anyone about it?"

"No, I haven't. You sounded ominous the other day. Was not like you. I told no one," said Sahr.

"You remember Mustafa Korafa, the one-time head of the intelligence service."

"Of course, he tried to rape my first wife. I told my mother's cousin, the Minister, about the incident. Korafa was obsessed with her, apparently, and thought our separation made her available. He went too far. We had him sent to run a prison in the north. If he had not known so much about the government in his intelligence position, he would probably have been sacked from everything, expelled, sent into exile, whatever. What has happened to him?"

"It appears you did not know he got the job of head of security at the Embassy in Washington. Well, his stay there was short-lived. I was ambassador there when Korafa showed up. I was encouraged to take him, although I didn't really have much choice. He had done his time with the prison. He was good at Security, all of that. Well, within weeks of his arrival, he was caught pursuing your wife; we believed he had hired someone to actually kill her. We had no proof of that. The FBI and State Department showed me pictures of him along with a couple of thugs breaking into her apartment building in New York. He had to go. We sent him back. The President had him discharged from government service. No one seems to know what he is doing now."

"I did not know that, Manu. Korafa tried to have Jenny killed? In New York? What are you telling me?" Sahr was incredulous.

"You didn't know. Well, the same Minister of the Interior, Agya, your mother's cousin, was advised of it. She must have known. No one told you?" asked Nrumah.

"No, no one told me, Manu," responded Sahr. I will have to speak with her, he thought. She wanted Jenny as far away from me as possible, but this has gone too far. "This is something I will have to deal with, my friend. You have something else to tell me. What is it?"

"Korafa had a deputy in the days he was head of intelligence. Wilson Kuma. The two of them have stayed in touch. You must know that Korafa harbors a deep resentment of what you brought on him years ago in relation to his attack on your wife. He has told people that the Akala family will pay for it someday. He thought he had an opportunity to take revenge on her in New York. He most probably will be trying to exact revenge on you. This brings me to the other matter. I was informed last week that Wilson Kuma works for your mother."

"Works for my mother? Doing what?"

"Special assignments. Protecting the family interests."

What is she up to? thought Sahr. Disturbing. "How do you know all this? What is really going on here?"

"What is going on, Sahr, is that Wilson Kuma has been enlisted by the President's people to report on the affairs of your family with the intention of breaking its political hold on the north. The President - and I know this because of my relations with people close to him - needs details of the various practices that your family and its man in Cabinet have employed to increase the family's fortunes over the years. Kuma has been turned - turned to report on your mother and the other members of the family on the political side. I must say he was blackmailed into it. He has some skeletons in his own closet. Do you want me to go on? This is about protecting yourself."

"Yes, go on. Tell me everything."

"You, as the animal doctor in the family, have been spared the scrutiny of the President. But it is your family, Sahr. If the Akala family comes down, you will come down with it. With the turning of Kuma, and the continued existence of his buddy Korafa somewhere in the background with the threat of revenge, the Akala family should be very worried."

Sahr leaned back and said nothing. He didn't know what to say. All he could think about was how his mother had ruined his marriage, his life, and now was in the process of having the family lose everything. She wrecked my marriage with the woman I loved. She forced him me to marry an innocent, illiterate young girl who never was and never could be a replacement for Jenny. All for the family.

"What do I do about this, Manu?"

"I don't know. I wish I did. The trouble is coming, Sahr. Just prepare yourself. Organize your affairs."

"Thank you, my friend," replied Sahr Akala as he rose from the table. He had heard enough.

26

In early 1993, Sahr was diagnosed with an advanced case of leukemia. Sisi, the youngest of his daughters, was in her last year of high school, while Efe, the oldest, was at university in England and was told to come home. The girls were informed that their father did not have long to live. In Yendi, while looking through some of her father's papers requested by the hospital, Efe discovered in the back of a drawer in his office a bundle of envelopes kept together by a rubber band and addressed to her and Sisi. Of the fourteen envelopes in the bundle, only two of them had been opened. Efe quickly saw the Accra return address in the corner of the envelopes with her mother's name. She took the letter from the first opened envelope and read it. It was dated April 10, 1980.

My dear Efe and Sisi,

I hope you are well. I love you dearly. I will be back with you soon. As I have said in my other letters to you, I have to be away for awhile, but I am not gone. I have not abandoned you. I am still in Ghana and will be back with you. Don't forget to brush your teeth. Love you.

Mommy

Efe opened up the other envelopes. The message was very much the same. *I have not abandoned you and will be back.*

"Daddy, what really happened to Momma?" asked Efe when alone with her father in the hospital room. She did not mention the discovery of her mother's letters, but soon would in the discussion they were having that day.

"She left, Efe. She couldn't live here. She was too used to America."

"No, she didn't, Daddy. She was in Accra a long time after she left here. Why was that? What did she do? Why was she there and not with us?.... She tried to contact us last year. When we were in school. Somebody from the American Embassy came and asked us if we would like to see our mother. I said no. We said no. I regretted it after. I had Sisi promise to say nothing about it."

"Efe, she abandoned us. She just left one day and we never heard from her," replied her father.

"Daddy, I know that is not true. What happened? I must know."

"How can you claim that is not true? Who has told you this? And how is it you did not tell me of the visit at the school?" Sahr was surprised at this. He had understood the school principal was to inform them of these things.

"I found a bundle of letters in the back of one of your office drawers, Daddy. From thirteen years ago. They were addressed to Sisi and I. Mommy said she was in Accra and would be coming back to us. That she had not abandoned us. Why were we never shown these letters? How many more have there been? Why have you kept them from us?"

Sahr Akala knew at that moment that the secret was up. He could not cover it up any longer. Tears filled his eyes as he looked at the distraught face of his beautiful eldest daughter who had just discovered the treachery of her father and his family. He did not have long to live. He decided at that moment to tell Efe what had happened.

"Efe, I will tell you. You must promise me one thing. though. That you not share what I tell you with your sister or with your grandmother until after I am gone. I can see the distress in your eyes. I can handle yours I think, but not of yours and Sisi's and my mother's all at the same time. But you must know."

"In the years in America when you were little, I had become more American than African, more American than Muslim. I had lost my identity. I loved your mother, but I did not love myself. I was a wayward soul. When we came here, I realized how African I really was, and how much of a Muslim I really was. Continuing to live here as we lived in America was a sham. It was not me. I was living a lie. Your mother expected us to be like we were when we were in America. It was not her fault, but I was torn. I could not keep living the same life. I was not me. That alone, though, was not enough to cause the disruption of my relationship with your mother. It may have in time, but not then. I still loved her."

"There was something else that came along that broke it all up, Efe. That something else along with my unhappiness with myself led to your mother leaving."

Sahr paused a moment, then continued with a feeble voice, belying his condition. "Our family was and still is, part of the political life of the country. Politics means clans, tribes, influence, power, government business. When in the midst of political life here, as in most of Africa, you cannot avoid having to do things to protect the interests of the family, of your clan." Sahr coughed, then continued. "We Akalas and particularly the family of your grandmother, with such a history of involvement in the affairs of the country going back to independence, were in danger of being shut out of government in 1979. A lot was at stake. My father's business, his influence in the community. The Akalas could be ruined unless we succeeded in solidifying our political standing. My mother spoke to me for months of taking a second wife, the daughter of the leader of the leading clan in Tamale and a fellow Muslim, to protect our interests. I resisted. I knew what it would do to your mother. There would be no way she would accept that. When she was away in Ohio looking after her parents' affairs after their deaths, a family council established that I had to take the young woman from Tamale as second wife. I was told it had to be done. If not, all could be lost. The Tamale clan, if rebuffed, would have most certainly gone another way and would have been powerful enough to exclude my father from any government business. I could not refuse. If I did, we would have to go back to America. I could not have faced my family. It was the African way or no way. From that second marriage with Ankela, you must know enough influence was gained to have your grandmother's cousin made Minister of the Interior, the most powerful position in the country next to the President. We have been very prosperous ever since. I know it means nothing to you now.....Your mother was the victim of all that. I have never forgiven myself for it. I hope you can."

"Momma has not been the only victim, Daddy."

"I'm sorry."

"Where is she?"

"I don't know. I received a letter from her years ago, but I threw it away. I understand she has lived in New York. I don't know any more than that, my dear." Sahr refrained from telling his daughter about what he had learned of the attempt on her mother's life.

"Were there other letters?"

"Yes, Efe. There were. For years, every month. I don't know where they are. After awhile, we ordered the post office here to destroy them when they came in. I'm sorry."

Later that evening, Sahr called for his eldest daughter. He was in his bed and knew he was dying. "Efe, I have something I want you to give your mother when you find her. You are going to search for her, aren't you?"

"Yes, Daddy, I am going to look for her."

"Here it is, Efe. I have no doubt you will find her. Even if it is not fresh anymore, give it to her for me." Sahr Akala held out a yellow rose on a long stem and gave it his daughter.

Sahr died the next day. His daughters, his second wife and his mother were with him when he died. His last regard before losing consciousness was one directed deep into the eyes of his eldest daughter.

27

"Sisi, our mother didn't abandon us. She has tried to reach us for years, ever since she left when we were little. Daddy told me everything two days ago. We didn't know any of it when the American talked to us at school," said Efe to her younger sister. "I'm going to try to find her."

"What? She has tried to reach us? How? We have never received anything. What are you talking about?'"

"Letters, Sisi. Every month for years. Intercepted by Daddy and Mama and destroyed. I found fourteen of them that were not destroyed in a packet in Daddy's papers at home. I was looking for stuff the hospital required. I brought them to him. He told me everything. Had me promise not to tell you before he died."

"I want to see them. Where are they?" said Sisi.

"Right here. In my purse."

Sisi Akala took the letters and read three or four of them. She looked up at Efe. Efe looked back at her younger sister, seeing the doubt in her eyes. The younger one had always been closer to her father and her grandmother. Efe knew that this would hurt. But it wasn't a hurt look in Sisi's eyes that she saw. It was a look of defiance, of disbelief. "So, what are you going to do? Try to find her?...I really don't care, Efe. Daddy is gone. I will do nothing to anger Mama. You do what you want. Our mother was never a part of our life. I don't believe she was forced out of the house and away from us when we were little. I don't care about the letters. A bunch of letters. Every month for years? Thrown away so we would not see them? Daddy was not like that. Mama would not do such a thing."

"Sisi, this is what Daddy told me two days ago," said Efe.

"I don't care. What do you want me to do? Go ask Mama what she did? I won't. For me, our mother is gone. Has always been gone. You can do what you want."

Efe Akala returned to university in England a few days later. One of the first things she did upon her return was call the New York City telephone listing service and ask if there was a Jennifer Sutton or a Jennifer Sutton Akala listed in the city. The operator said there was a listing for a Jennifer Sutton who lived at an address in Brooklyn. Efe called the number, reached the lady who said that no, she was not the person the young lady was looking for. She had lived in New York all her life and had been retired from teaching for fifteen years. Efe called the telephone company once again, asking this time if there were any J. Suttons. The operator said there were nine and gave Efe the numbers for all of them. Efe called every one that evening. Four answered. They were not the J. Sutton she was looking for. Two were John Suttons, one was Janet Sutton and the other did not want to say. She called and reached the five others over the next two days. Same result. No number for Mom in New York. Where is she? How do I do this?

Efe could not know that her mother had left the city the year before and had her phone service discontinued. The couple who rented her apartment had their own number.

After being back in England for three weeks, Efe received word in a call from her grandmother that the family had arranged for Sisi to marry a young man from the Tamale region. The wedding would take place sometime after Sisi's graduation from high school in Accra. News of the date would follow.

The letter from Efe to her sister contained one line, "Are you happy, Sisi? If you are, I am happy for you. Your sis, Efe." The elder of the two Akala sisters never received a reply to the letter.

A few weeks later, Efe was invited by Kate Wilson, a friend at the University of Sheffield, to spend a weekend at the Wilson family cottage in Oxfordshire. She readily accepted. Efe lived with a cousin of her father who had been established in England for many years and worked in research at the University. Her father had been an undergraduate there. She had met Kate soon after arriving and the two became close friends. The weekend visit would be the first encounter of Efe with her friend's family. The cottage and the small estate around it was the property of Kate's grandfather, Geoffrey Wilson, recently retired from management at NewsWorld Magazine. Efe had no idea that the weekend in the country would change her life.

"Where are you from, my dear? I understand it is Ghana, but I had Zambia in my head for some reason when Kate told us she had a friend coming for the weekend," asked the man with the thick, wavy, silver-gray hair in the debonair style of the British upper-class.

"I'm from Ghana, Mr. Wilson. From a small town in the Northeast of the country called Yendi. My father was the area's veterinarian until his recent death."

"And your mother, Efe? You are not totally African, if I may say so." Efe Akala had skin of a mid-brown color with facial features that were more Caucasian than African.

"My mother was American," responded Efe.

"You say was. I take it she is no longer around. What happened to her, if I may ask?" said Geoffrey Wilson as they sat in the cottage's garden room overlooking the lawn at the back of the property.

"Well, I say 'was' because she has been out of our lives since I was five years old. There is a complicated story to it, Mr. Wilson. I am actually trying to find her, but with no luck to date."

Geoffrey Wilson had a thought. Could this be related to what Peterson had submitted years ago? American woman in Ghana cut off from her children?

"Miss Akala… Efe. Could you tell me more about this? Is it something you wish to share?" asked Geoffrey. "If you would prefer not, it would be quite alright. But I can see this is very important to you." After a short pause, he continued. "It could be that I may be able to help you."

"Well, if you wish. I have only discovered recently that my mother did not abandon my younger sister and me as we were told. My father admitted to me just before his death that he had expelled my mother from the home, eventually causing her to leave Ghana and return to the United States. I discovered letters to my sister and I in my father's papers before he died that clearly established she wanted to be with us. I have been quite upset about it. Upset with my father, with my grandmother as well who had much to do with the banishment of my mother. It has been thirteen years."

"I'm sorry to hear that, Efe," replied Geoffrey Wilson. This is the family from the Peterson story. I'm sure of it. It was real after all. "What has happened? From what you say I assume you are going to pursue this further."

"There is more to it, if you don't mind my speaking of it, Mr. Wilson. Two years ago, well before I found the letters and had confronted my father with what I had discovered, Sisi, my sister and I were contacted by someone from the United States Embassy who was inquiring if we wanted to see our mother. We had always understood she had abandoned us. That was not the case, but we did not know that at the time, and told the Embassy person we were not interested. The pain over the years had been too great, particularly when we were little. If only I would have known. I am looking for her now."

Yes, Peterson's Lady from Toledo. Geoffrey Wilson leaned forward towards the young lady in front of him. "I know of this, young lady. Much of your story, I'm afraid. I will tell you why. But I can tell you how you can perhaps find your mother. I have a good idea of where you can start."

"But how, Mr. Wilson? How could you possibly be aware of this?" asked Efe.

"I was the international editor for NewsWorld magazine for many years. In 1981, I received a story for publication as a special feature from our lead African correspondent. It was a story about a lady he had met who had lost access to her children in Africa. An American lady who had gone to Ghana with her Ghanaian husband after marrying in the United States, and had been expelled from the home with no contact allowed with her children. Our man had met the lady, who I believe now was your mother. Unfortunately, the correspondent had only sparse sources of information for the story, with no one in Ghana willing to substantiate what he was saying. Plus, there was sensitive material in it that had more to do with politics than with your mother. I turned it down. I could not corroborate anything that the correspondent had put in his article. He was very upset when I canned it and soon left the magazine."

Geoffrey Wilson continued. "I know where he is working now. He could possibly have kept in touch with your mother. One never knows about these things. Do you want to pursue this, Efe?"

"Yes, I do, Mr. Wilson. I think we are both talking about my mother. This is quite incredible. My friendship with Kate, this weekend, your involvement years ago. Quite an improbable connection. Yes, definitely. Who is the person you are talking about and where can I reach him?"

"His name is Jay Peterson. He is with NewsMag Media now. I see his byline on stories from time to time. Let me go to my desk. I will get you the number in New York."

"Here it is. I hope you reach him," said the elderly man, "and I hope you find your mother."

The next afternoon Efe called NewsMag Media Corporation in New York. "Could I speak with Jay Peterson, please?"

"Just a moment," replied the telephone receptionist.

Good. Looks like he still works there, thought Efe.

"Hello, this is Jay Peterson. Please leave me a detailed message and I will get back to you as soon as possible," said the recorded message.

"Hello, Mr. Peterson. This is Efe Akala. I am looking for my mother, Jennifer Sutton Akala. I am informed you may possibly know where she is or how I can reach her. If you in any way can help with that, please call me. I would like to find her. I am calling from Sheffield, England. It is Monday afternoon, the 14th of April. Here is the number where I am. You can reach me anytime in the evening." Efe ended the message and hung up the phone.

Jay Peterson picked up his messages later that day. He could not believe what he was hearing. Jenny's daughter calling from England. Wants to know where she is. Good lord, here we go.....Breakthrough. Yes. But how in the world did she know I might be able to connect her with her mother? Jay looked at his watch - 3:30. 8:30 in England. Miss Akala, how I am anxious to speak with you. He dialed the number.

"Hullooo." The baritone voice at the other end was deep with a heavy accent.

"Hello, I am trying to reach Efe Akala. I am returning her call of earlier today."

"Just a moment. I will fetch her," replied the male voice.

"Hello, this is Efe. Who is calling?"

"Efe, this is Jay Peterson. I am calling from New York. I received your message of earlier today. You are looking for your mother."

"Yes, I am, Mr. Peterson. I am trying to reach her. I have not seen my mother in close to fourteen years. I want to re-establish contact with her. I am informed you may know where she is."

"Yes, I do. It is not New York, however. How did you get my name, Efe? I will be able to help you with your request, but how did you learn that I may know your mother?"

"I met the grandfather of a university friend of mine here in England this past weekend. His name is Geoffrey Wilson. When he asked me about my family in Ghana, I told him my story. He told me he knew someone who may be able to help. He said you wrote an article years ago about an American woman in Ghana who had been separated from her children. He believes the story was about my mother, that he was aware of where you worked now, and that I should get in touch with you."

Geoffrey Wilson. I'll be damned, thought Jay while the young lady was speaking. What a connection. I don't believe this.

"Efe, this is quite something. I do know a lot about your mother. It is a long story. There was an article I wrote about her - twelve years ago. It never got published. But I have been in contact with her in recent years. I must say she has been in despair of ever seeing you and your sister again. She made many attempts to reach you. I'm not sure you are aware of that."

"I haven't been, Mr. Peterson. But I am now. All contact with my mother was forbidden and all communications intercepted. My father admitted that to me the day before he died. Where is she? Do you know where she is?"

"As I told you, she is not here, unfortunately, Efe. She left New York a few months ago. She is in India, working with a school for girls in a remote part of the country. I do not have a number there nor an address, I'm afraid. But there is someone who can assist you in finding her. That person actually is in London. I can put you in touch with her."

"Please do, Mr. Peterson. Who is she?"

"Her name is Margaret Bishop and by this time tomorrow I will have a telephone number for you," said Jay. "How old are you now, Efe?"

"I'm twenty.".

"We will find your mother for you. She is going to be overjoyed when she sees you. To say the least. She has spent the years since you were a child in anguish. It will be some reunion."

The next day, Jay called Efe in Sheffield. "Efe, here is Margaret Bishop's number in London. Call her. As I said, she can tell you where your mother went to in India. In the meantime, I will be in London two weeks from now to follow up on a story I am writing. I could come up to where you are or we could meet in London. I would like to meet you. I will share with you what I know of what your mother has gone through all these years. It will help you when you ultimately find her, which I am sure you will. Do we do that?"

"Yes, Mr. Peterson. I would very much appreciate that. Thank you. I will be calling Margaret Bishop tomorrow, and I would be most happy to travel to London to see you."

"All the best, Efe. We will speak soon." Jay hung up the phone. My God. This is going to happen.

28

She had been there a few months. The school was indeed in a remote part of India, very much cut off from the mainstream development in the country. It was poor, and the school reflected it. Whatever limited resources it had were provided by the U.K. through the High Commission in Delhi. Jenny had been warmly welcomed by the school's principal and teachers. It was organized and well staffed, however, she had little to do, other than dealing with the High Commission and occasional administrative matters. Teaching was out of the question, as Hindi was the language of use. English was beyond the reach of the girls there, many of whom were from the lowest classes of society. Jenny had lots of free time. Through a colleague, she got into meditation and ended up spending time every day meditating. She found a car for sale in a nearby village, a Czech-made Skoda and used it to travel around. To avoid problems, she had a local boy become her driver and bodyguard, so to speak. The young man was barely five foot four inches tall, but was street-smart, knew how to drive and spoke English. It was enough. Jenny, at five foot ten, was an imposing looking lady to begin with. Nobody bothered her and her little bodyguard as they travelled around in her free time.

After three months, Jenny sent a letter to her boss in New York, telling him it would probably be another six months before she returned to New York. She said she hoped he understood and would let him know her return plans well in advance. She was not ready to return to the world of New York. Advertising.

Madison Avenue. The city. No. No more of that. I really should tell him. Maybe another letter.

Jenny was bored after another month and believed she could be better spending her time elsewhere. She thought of what Tim Hurley had told her about the Laotian girl he had helped exit a dreary existence in a refugee camp. He had given her the name of the place. Somdet Ya, twenty kilometers west of the town of Nong Kai, across the Mekong from Laos, and reachable by bus or car from Bangkok. Somdet Ya. Maybe I can be of better use there.

Somdet Ya, April 1993.....

Every house with a Buddha out front. The smell of incense. Little ceremony in front of the Buddha every day, every house. Nice. I could like it here, she thought. Jenny had arrived two days before and had found a room at the town's only hotel, a structure sitting above ground on pillars of teak, with rooms separated by bamboo curtains. There were no locks. Clients slept on mats spread on spotless, polished floors. They were invited to leave their valuables with the owners who had a closed room and a safe. It was the only place for lodging, unless one was invited by a resident to stay with them. Lovely, thought Jenny as she explored what the village and the area were all about.

From Nong Kai, she had taken a 'bus' to the village. It was a pick-up truck with seats in the back. Patrons told the driver where they wanted to go and he drove them there. Door to door service. There were scooters everywhere, along with the pick-up trucks and 4-wheel drives that were the vehicles of preference. Chickens and pigs had to be avoided and an occasional water buffalo could be seen not far off the road. The Mekong was nearby and occasionally overran its banks in the rainy season.

There were orchids everywhere. Despite the heat, kids were dressed for school. They all had uniforms. Everything and everyone were clean. She saw that many of the boys were dressed as Buddhist monks, with orange robes and shaved heads. She would learn later that studying to be a monk was often the only way for poorer parents to have their sons educated. They would get an education in the monastery; serve for a few years, then in most cases leave.

On her second day in the village, before she had the chance to enquire about the internment camp, even if it still existed, she was introduced to the festivities of the Thailand water holiday. Towards the end of the afternoon, she heard shrieks of people and load music and walked to the center of the village to see what was going on. She was surprised to see dozens of people being hosed with water and reciprocating as fast as they could. Barrels of water were being emptied on people's heads, music was blaring from loudspeakers, people were laughing while being doused and dousing others in turn, with buckets being dipped in huge tanks in the center of the town square. Everybody was soaked but obviously having a great time.

"What is this? Do you speak English?" she asked a young girl.

"Yes, I speak English. It is the Songkran festival. Water holiday. All over Thailand it is like this."

Jenny turned quickly as she felt someone approaching, only to receive the full contents of a large bucket of water dumped on her. The woman who did it said something to Jenny. As Jenny was shaking off the water from her hair and wiping her face, she asked the young girl what the woman had said.

"She said 'welcome to Somdet Ya'."

"OK, how do I become part of this?"

"Come with me. There are buckets over there."

She got one, filled it up, found the woman who had doused her and unloaded the bucket on her, with both proceeding to laugh and do it all again.

The next day, Jenny found someone who could tell her about the camp for the Lao. She was given directions and found a 'bus' to take her there. She got into the back of the truck and off they went, a few kilometers up the bank of the river. She discovered that the place was still one of detention. People were not free to come and go. There was a fence with a gate with armed soldiers. Through the bus driver who understood English, Jenny asked a guard if she could go inside or speak with an administrator. She was told that was not possible. She would have to have permission from authorities in Nong Kai. The place was off limits to foreigners.

That evening Jenny ran into an Australian woman at one of the outdoor food stalls in the center of the village, one of the few Europeans one could find in Somdet Ya. Jenny asked her if she knew anything about the camp. She related that she had a friend who told her the story of someone who had been detained there and was curious about what it was all about. "I am traveling around Southeast Asia. I heard there was a detention center for Laotian refugees....Why would there still be one by the way? The wars here were over twenty years ago."

The woman said she was aware of one in the region, but suggested that if Jenny wanted to know more, there was an

International Red Cross representative in Nong Kai. The office was on the main square.

"People don't talk about that here. Thais and Lao are not traditional friends. It goes back a long time."

"Ah, I see. Maybe I should learn more about that." Jenny paused briefly, then continued. "Thank you for the tip. We should get together some time. I'm staying down the road there - the little hotel on stilts."

"Very good. I have a house down there," pointing off to the left. "My partner and I have been here four years now. We spend the Australian winters here. We are getting to know the place pretty well."

Jenny took the pick-up bus into Nong Kai the next day and managed to meet the representative of the Red Cross, a New Zealander. "Hello, my name is Derek," said the man who looked to be in his mid-thirties. "How can I help you?"

"Derek, my name is Jennifer. I was told a few years ago of the Lao refugee camp at Somdet Ya by a friend. He had deplored what he knew of the conditions there and suggested that the place could use a proper school for girls. I have just come from India where I worked with one for orphaned girls. I founded one in Ghana years ago, and I have worked extensively with a center in Harlem back in New York. If the place at Somdet Ya has a school, perhaps I could help."

"I see," replied the New Zealander.

Jerry continued with her questions. "Is there a school at the camp? What do you know of it, if there is one? Is it worth exploring? I don't know anyone else here to ask these questions. By the way, I'm not looking to be paid. I have taken a leave of absence from a job in the United States. I am not in need of money."

"Well, it is not often someone shows up who offers to help around here," said Derek. "There is a school for girls there. I'm sure the people who run it would be interested. They don't have much money, so not requesting any compensation would be appreciated. It is run by a Christian group, Baptist I believe, and they don't do a bad job of it. I could put you in touch with the headmaster. I know her. She's a nice lady. From Oklahoma, I believe. And where are you from?"

"Ohio...but many years gone from there. Baptists, you say," said Jenny. "Very good. I would appreciate it if you could introduce me to the lady."

"Very well. I have the number somewhere here. They have a telephone. Peggy Nash.....Peggy Nash. Here it is. Do you want me to call her? We can do it now."

Jenny Sutton and Peggy Nash met the next day. They met at the gate and proceeded in the lady's pick-up to the school. Jenny made an arrangement for the bus driver to retrieve her at 4 pm.

"I would be glad to have you here. We can always use help. We have five teachers. There is space for three hundred girls. We work two shifts a day, two hours each day each shift. It's the best we can do. The girls learn how to read and write in the Thai language and in English. Enough arithmetic to get them by. They learn Thai because they are not going back to Laos, at least 90% of them won't. You could perhaps help us with English and with arithmetic. Pretty basic, but needed here. There is no other source of schooling for them. With it, they have a chance to get out, find a job and move on. Many of the girls when they get to be fifteen or sixteen escape and go to Bangkok and become party girls, the Thai version of prostitution. Bangkok is full of pretty young girls who have escaped places like this, do the thing in Pat-Pong Road, Pattaya and other places, helped in doing so by boys who have learned how to take advantage of it. You and I would call them pimps back home."

"I know a bit about that. The friend who told me of this place years ago met a girl who escaped from here and had her accepted as a refugee in Canada. Has a family there now. Saved her. What about the girls who are orphans? Is there a place for them here?" asked Jenny

"Not really. They become slaves, if you will, for families who accept to take them in. Work in exchange for a roof over their head. Not nice."

"No wonder they want to leave," said Jenny.

"Yes, no wonder."

"Is it something that could be considered - a hostel for the orphaned girls? Get them out of the slavery stuff? Would that be possible?" asked Jenny.

"If the money could be found, anything is possible. With Derek in Nong Kai, we could perhaps get the Red Cross involved, as long as there was another source or two of funding. It's not impossible. We would need a building. Nothing for that exists here at the moment."

"Something we could perhaps work on, Peggy. In the meantime, if you want me for the school, I'm in."

"Great, I'm happy about this."

"I'll be here tomorrow if you wish," said Jenny. "I imagine there is no place for me to stay here."

"Well, there isn't, but you don't want to stay within these confines to begin with. I live in the village. Come in every day. You will want to do the same. But, yes, see you tomorrow. We can work on a plan for your participation."

Jenny did a bit of a contract with the bus driver later that afternoon for daily trips, starting the next day.

"The reality for the people here is bleak, Jenny. The school is the one bright spot for the kids, at least the ones we can accommodate. We can take maybe 2/3's of the school age girls who are here. My priority with Derek is getting some funding for two more class rooms. It would give us another 120 spaces. The Lao have little to do here. They eat, sleep, and kill time. The Thai government built the living quarters here years ago, but have not kept pace with improvements or maintenance. They provide food but are always pressuring the international aid organizations to give money, even take over responsibility, but do not want people leaving. They hope they will go back to Laos. That is not possible for most of them. The war left its traces. The regime is Communist over there and does not take kindly to their people who left and want to come back. It is at a standstill. People are just stuck here."

"Most people spend their time socializing with friends. Some people find sewing machines and make clothes - little businesses dependent upon somehow getting a machine. Many

186

people pass their time **by playing a local version of** soccer with a rattan ball, using a volleyball net for a goal. Get the ball over the net however you can, except with your hands. People are allowed to fish in the Mekong, which is not far away. But they must come back. They need passes to leave. A pass allows one person to leave for a few hours, but he or she has to be back before midnight. There are quotas. Only twenty passes a day are issued. People have to get in line for them. The line every day is a long one. That is life here."

"Why do you do this, Peggy?" enquired Jenny.

"Good question. The love of God, I suppose." The little Baptist lady looked over at Jenny who had a skeptical look on her face, paused, then continued "I see bright faces here and I believe we are doing something really good. And, I have little to go back to in Oklahoma. I will tell you about it sometime."

29

"Hello….Margaret Bishop here. What can I do for you?" Margaret was at her office in London.

"Mrs. Bishop, this is Efe Akala. I believe you know my mother, Jennifer Sutton. I was told you may be aware of where she is. I am trying to find her."

Margaret could hardly believe what she had just heard. "My God! What a surprise. Young lady, I would be glad to help you find her. Who brought you to me, my dear?"

"Jay Peterson, a man in New York. I spoke with him yesterday. I am in Sheffield. I go to university here. It has been a long time regarding my mother. Many things have happened that have kept us apart."

"I know a lot of that, my dear. I would like to see you. Could you come to London? In the meantime, I can tell you your mother is in India. She has been there for six months now. A place that is difficult to reach, in one of the poorest parts of the country." She paused a moment, then continued. "Jay Peterson, the journalist, New York. How in the world were you put in touch with him?"

"It's a long story, Mrs. Bishop. I can speak about that should I see you. I will be meeting Mr. Peterson in London in two weeks. I can meet you on the same trip into the city. I could let you know when I am coming. In the meantime, what is the town or the city my mother is in India?"

"She is helping with a **school** for lower caste girls in a small village a few miles from the town of Manawar. It is in the southwest part of the central Indian state of Madhya Pradesh. I have the address where you can write to her, but I am afraid there is no telephone where she is," said Margaret.

"I don't want to write to her," replied Efe. "I want to go find her, to see her. India....I can go there once the term is over."

"Very good, Efe, but I must tell you, where she is is very much out of the way."

"That's all right. I will find a way to get there. I'm going to do it."

"We can talk about it when I see you," replied Margaret. "If you do this, I will have people in Delhi help you."

"I will see you soon, Mrs. Bishop. Thank you for this."

Two evenings later....

The phone rang at the house in Sheffield. It was her grandmother, calling from Yendi. "So, you are trying to reach your mother. What is this about, Efe? What has gotten into you? She abandoned you when you were a child." Efe knew immediately what had happened. My uncle - he overheard my discussion with Mr. Peterson. He answered the telephone that evening.

"Yes, I am, Mama. I am trying to reach my mother. I am determined to find her. You must know that Father told me everything the day before he died. She did not abandon us. The letters that were kept from Sisi and I all that time. What happened

189

when she left Yendi. Everything. He was sorry. He said he loved our mother. It was a mistake. He regretted it."

"Efe, no. You will not do this. Your father was sick. The truth is something else," replied Madame Akala.

"I will do it, Mama. You can't stop me. I am here, not in Ghana."

"If you persist in this, I will stop the money. You will have to leave university. I will not allow it, Efe. You will no longer be welcome in your uncle's house in Sheffield. I will do it."

"There is something you are obviously not aware of, Mama. Father provided me with enough money to finish university and more. After the burial in Yendi, his assistant at the clinic brought me an envelope. In it was a bank draft for 40,000 pounds. There was a note. It said "I believe you may need this someday, my dear. Don't spend it until you have to. It was signed 'Love you, Father'. It is sitting in a bank account here in England. I don't need your money, Mama. I am going to find my own Momma. I'm sorry. Good-bye." By the end of the afternoon the following day, Efe had moved in with Kate Wilson's family.

London, two weeks later

Jay Peterson very much wanted to meet Jenny's daughter. They made plans to meet in the lobby of his hotel. Here she comes. Must be her. Afro. Milk chocolate skin. Tall. Elegant. Soft eyes. Beautiful. Jenny's daughter.

"Mr. Peterson? Is it you?" asked the young woman as she approached Jay, who had stood up to greet her.

"Yes, that's me. Very nice to meet you, Efe. You look a lot like your mother, by the way."

"I have no idea of that, Mr. Peterson. I don't really remember what she looked like. All the pictures of her were taken from us."

"Well, she is tall, like you. Frizzy hair. Lighter skin, though" - they both laughed - "big dark eyes, an elegant way about her. You are like her," said Jay.

"How did you meet my mother? I take it you are a friend of hers now."

"What do you know, Efe, of the circumstances of your mother's time in Accra, after you were separated? That is where I met her, in 1981."

"I know very little of that. All I know is that mother was expelled, how else can I say it, from our home by my father. He told me what really happened just before he died a few weeks ago. We had always been told she had left the home on her own - abandoned us. It was not true. But he told me nothing of her time in Accra. All I am aware of is what Mr. Wilson told me about a magazine piece you had written about her - you apparently had met her somehow - something that never got published. He did not tell me very much else."

"There is a lot to the story of your mother, Efe. Some of it is not very nice. Not very nice about your country and not very nice about my own country as well, for that matter."

"Tell me. I want to hear it," said Efe. "I know now that her absence from my life and the life of my sister was not of her doing. Tell me. Please."

"Very well. There is a lot to it. I was introduced to your mother by a Canadian - a consultant who had met your mother through a common American friend......." Jay told her all he knew of her mother's life since the separation years before. It took the better part of an hour. Efe was silent, taking it all in, her face one of sadness, melancholy, and tears she would gently wipe away while Jay Peterson told her of her mother's life away from her and her sister.

"Threatened? Almost raped? Intercepted on her way to try to see us, prevented from coming? Almost murdered in New York? All because she wanted to see us? She didn't abandon us at all. My father told me some of it, but none of what you have been telling me. We had no idea. My God.......how cruel. We never knew," whispered the young lady as she gazed at the man across from her with tears in her eyes.

"No, she didn't abandon you, Efe. Your welfare and reuniting with you has been the center of her life ever since she was forced to leave. Despondent, pursued and stalked, all of that. She wrote letters to you every month with no replies. They were all intercepted."

"Yes, my father admitted it," said Efe.

"She received no assistance from the U.S. Government. The office in Accra did nothing to help her. After I met your mother in Accra I decided to write her story." Jay paused a moment before continuing. "There were other things going on in the country at the time that compromised the U.S. Government, making it an interesting tale on more than one account. Geoffrey, my good old friend Geoffrey at the time, the same Geoffrey Wilson you met recently, turned it down. I was very upset. I left the magazine over it." Jay decided that he would not speak of what he knew of the politics and machinations of the young

192

lady's grandmother's family. She would perhaps learn of that in time, but he decided it would not come from him.

"Have you seen her recently?" asked Efe.

"A few months ago. Just before she left for India. Got a postcard just before Christmas. No news since."

"I am going to find her. I am meeting with Margaret Bishop this evening. She has invited me to her house in Ealing for dinner and I will be staying the night. Says she has a parrot that belonged to my mother in Accra. Name of Buckeye. What is a buckeye, Mr. Peterson? Strange name for a bird."

"Not if you are from Ohio. It's the name of the football team of the university your mother went to."

"Thank you for leading me to Mrs. Bishop. She has told me where mother is. I must leave now. Have to get to the tube. Thank you for everything. I hope we meet again."

"I hope we do too. All the best. Good luck in your search. I'm sure you will find her. All the best." Jay rose and gave Efe Akala a big hug. "Please forgive me. This is not very Muslim."

"I don't really care about that anymore, Mr. Peterson. We were never big on that. Ghana is not Saudi Arabia for one, plus I went to Catholic schools and am now at a British university. I am a long ways from all of that. Thank God. I was never impressed with the Muslim customs. They are not very nice for us women. Thank you again. I will let you know what happens."

Very much like her mother, thought Jay. I wonder what the father was like. The girl turned out pretty good. I hope this ends well.

"Sisi, your sister is not coming back here this summer. She is abandoning the family. She has been corrupted in England. She has left the house of your uncle. God knows where she is living. You will not do that, will you? You still love your Mama?"

"Yes, Mama. I still love you. My place is here. I have no desire to leave. Efe can do as she wishes. I will not follow her. Do not worry about that, Mama."

30

"You look a lot like your mother," said Margaret Bishop as she pulled away from the curb. She had waited at the Ealing tube station for the daughter of her old friend from Accra and immediately saw that the tallest of the women emerging from the station was the one who was coming to see her. Unmistakable.

"I was told that this afternoon as well, Mrs. Bishop. Thank you for having me," replied Efe as she looked over at the driver.

"You are quite welcome, my dear. I am anxious to tell you what I know of your mother and I must admit, am very curious about you and your life. I look forward to hearing it all from you. I liked your mother very much and still do."

Efe Akala and Margaret Bishop spent the next three hours talking about Efe's life, her family back in Ghana, and what Margaret knew of her mother and her mother's life, complementing what she had learned earlier that day from Jay Peterson. Efe learned the details of where her mother had gone to in India and received instructions on how to get there. There was no telephone at the school. Margaret counseled her to go first to the High Commission in Delhi and people there would direct her on the best way to reach the village. She had spoken with the High Commission the day before and was told that Jennifer Sutton was apparently still at the school, living there, and part of the staff, although unpaid, and they would facilitate her daughter's voyage. "I suggest you bring a friend with you, Efe. A male friend. You will need it. Not recommended for young women to travel alone in India."

"I will do it in July," said Efe. "I will go to India right after the last of the lectures. Two months away. It will give me time to recruit a bodyguard."

"Kate, who can I invite to come with me to India? I need a guy to come with me. Travel companion to ward off people with ill intent. Can't go there by myself. Know anybody? I can think of a couple of boys who have been in my classes, but they would not seem to be ideal." Efe had arrived that afternoon from London and the two of them were in the kitchen of the Wilson home in Sheffield.

"Hmmm....somebody who would be fun, but could be of a presence to discourage any trouble.....who would not expect sex, right?" replied Kate.

"Right. I'm not ready for any of that. But, yes, somebody who could be fun. Simon is out of the question," referring to the boy she had dated earlier that year.

Kate fetched a pad of paper and pen and went to the kitchen table. "Come on. Let's see what sort of a list we can come up with." The two friends spent the next hour compiling a list of young men from the university and qualifying them along a grid of five criteria - fun person to be with, manliness for deterrence, probability of unwanted sexual interest, reliability, probable level of interest in travelling to India. Scale of 1 to 5 for each criterion. Out of the twelve young men they put through the grid, five came to the top. It took two days, but they found the travel companion for Efe. Stewart Bell - 'Stewy' to the people who knew him and fourth on the list - accepted enthusiastically. Efe had found him in the lounge. "Good show, Ef" said Kate. "Stewy the Kiwi. Rugby player. Nobody will mess with him. He has a girl friend that we both know, and he is super nice. Good show. What about Lindy, his girlfriend?"

"He says it will be OK. She is going off to the States for the summer, and he was wondering what he would do. He didn't want to have to go back to Auckland for the whole summer, which is winter there. This solves the problem for him. I will meet him in Delhi in mid-July and we will go from there. Yes!"

New Delhi, late July 1993

"Miss Akala, your mother is no longer at the school." Pradeet, the Indian lady working at the High Commission was disconsolate. "We just received word last week that she had left a few months ago and had gone to Thailand. I'm sorry you came all this way simply to learn that, but we have but infrequent communications with the school. They do not have telephone service in the countryside there, and there is no ongoing reason for us to be in regular contact with them to begin with, although we do provide them with some annual funding. I am sorry. I was going to send a note this week to Margaret as we spoke about your coming here a few weeks ago. I had forgotten that you would be coming here at this time. I am truly sorry."

"Oh. Well, I'm not sure what to do now." Efe was clearly thrown off by what the lady was telling her. After a pause, she asked her "Do you know if they have an idea where she went in Thailand?"

"They did not say. You could go to the school and ask them but they may not have that. As I said, there is no telephone there. We can write to them and wait for a reply, but that could

197

take a week or more. If you would like to go there, there is train service to Bhopal, the state capital and bus service from there. I have taken it. It is not a difficult journey, just long. It will take you a day. But, if you do go, you will be taking a chance they may not know where she went."

"We'll go to Thailand," blurted Stewart.

"Well." Efe was not sure how to proceed."I think I will call Margaret. Maybe she would know someone who would have an idea of where she may have gone to. She has been in touch with friends of my mother over the years."

"Miss, I feel very bad about this. If you want to call Ms. Bishop in London, you can do it from here. Now, if you wish. It is mid-morning in London. We can perhaps reach her. Do you want to do that?"

"Yes, please," replied Efe.

"Margaret, this is Efe Akala. I am in Delhi, with Pradeet, the lady at the High Commission. She has just learned my mother is no longer with the school in the countryside. She left for Thailand a couple of months ago. Would you know where she could have gone to in Thailand, by chance?"

"Efe, I'm so sorry to hear that. If I had known that, I surely would have told you......Thailand, they said....... I have an idea. Where can I reach you in the next couple of days? I have a couple of telephone calls to make."

"I am with Stewart, my travel companion, at a hostel here in Delhi. I can leave you the number."

"Miss Akala, you have a telephone message from London." The receptionist gave Efe the note. "You can call from here. I will have to charge you five pounds for it, but you could perhaps ring the person and have her ring you back here at this number to save any other charges. Communications from here to the U.K. are expensive."

"Yes, please. Let's do that," replied Efe. A few moments later, Margaret Bishop returned the call. She had mentioned in her message she had some promising news before hanging up and ringing back.

"Efe, a friend of mine who also had met your mother when she was in Accra and who lives in Paris, knows a Canadian living in Boston who stayed in touch with your mother. He called him; his name is Tim Hurley and he gave Brian the information that your mother was probably at a place in northern Thailand."

"I will go there," replied Efe. "Efe, I will give you the number I have for Tim Hurley in Boston," said Margaret. "Brian assures me he would be glad to help you." Efe took down the number. "What time is it in Boston now? How many hours difference?"

"It is 4 PM in Delhi now, so it should be 5:30 in the morning in Boston. Wait a few hours. It is a weekday. Chances are Mr. Hurley will be at his office around 8 PM your time. Ring him then. Good luck. Let me know what happens."

She turned to Stewart who was beside her. "Are you OK with going to the north of Thailand? I have some money. I will pay for your ticket." Daddy's money. Will be put to good use, she thought. Stewart nodded and gave a thumbs-up.

At 8 PM, Efe rang the number in Boston and asked to be put through to Tim Hurley. She got a voicemail response and left a message. "Mr. Hurley, this is Efe Akala. Jennifer Sutton is my mother. I am in New Delhi, India, looking for her. I have been told she is now in Thailand, and that you may know where she has gone. Could I ask you to call me at this number in Delhi? It is the number of the youth hostel I am staying at."

Twenty minutes later, the receptionist at the hostel came running down the hall to the lounge where Efe and Stewart had gone to wait. "Ms. Akala, there is someone on the telephone asking for you. Please come to the desk."

"Efe, this is Tim Hurley. Brian Maxwell told me about your search for your mother. I must say I am very heartened you are doing this. Your mother has been in dismay for years. You probably know that by now."

"Yes, I do, Mr. Hurley. I very much want to find her."

"Very good. When Brian mentioned Thailand this morning, I immediately remembered the conversation I had with your mother last year about what I had experienced in Thailand regarding a refugee camp when I was working there years ago. She may have gone there. I would not be surprised. Somdet Ya, on the Mekong River across from the capital, Vientiane and near the town of Nong Khai. You can get there by bus from Bangkok. I suggest you not go there alone, however. A male companion would be best."

"Mr. Hurley, I thank you very much. I will go there. I have no other leads about where she could be. I have a bodyguard, by the way. No problem with that."

"Do not hesitate to get in touch with me if you have difficulty over there. You have my number. Leave me a message with how I can reach you. Good luck."

"Thank you. I will do so."

"Stewie, here we go," said Efe to her big male friend.

"Right on. I'm in. Never been to Thailand. Madame, where is the nearest travel agency?" Stewart said, turning to the receptionist.

Efe and Stewart found places on an Air India flight to Bangkok three days later. They spent the interim touring Delhi. There was much to see. Stewart managed to get tickets to an India-Pakistan cricket match that began the afternoon of their last day there. It could last two days they were told - cricket matches could be like that. The match only ended when they were on the plane to Bangkok. "Crazy, Stewie. Fans were nuts," said Efe later as they left the stadium. "India and Pakistan, my dear," replied Stewart. "Blood feud. Just like New Zealand and Australia in rugby."

By the time they arrived in Bangkok, they had become good friends and were enjoying each other's company. Efe talked about Africa and Stewart about New Zealand. They learned a lot about areas of the world they did not know much about beforehand. The plan was to find the bus station the next morning and take the first one available to Nong Khai. "I need to get there. I don't want to dally. I haven't seen my mother since I was six years old. I'm close now. I feel she is there. We need to go."

"No problem. I'm with you," he replied as they went out to find a restaurant. There were plenty nearby as they walked down side streets off the main boulevards that were full of chugging three wheel taxi 'put-puts'.

"Excited?" asked Stewie.

"Yes. Excited…and apprehensive."

"What's the first thing you are going to do when you see her?"

"Probably cry. Then….I don't know."

"Miss, the best time to take the bus north is at night. Not as hot. Less traffic. The one tonight leaves at 9:45, arrives in Nong Khai close to 8 in the morning. There are places still available."

"But what about today, buses leaving earlier than that?" asked Efe who was clearly impatient to get going.

"There are. There is one that leaves at 11, in three hours from now, and another at 2. They make many stops, however, and the voyage will take you fourteen hours. Each of them will bring you to Nong Khai late in evening. Not smart. I suggest you wait for the one tonight. Only two other stops."

Efe looked at Stewart, then at the lady. "We will go tonight. Two tickets to Nong Khai. Second class."

"There is no second class on that bus. Only first class. Big seats. Easy to sleep."

Efe and her Kiwi bodyguard arrived in Nong Khai the next morning. The bus terminal was a big, rambling, soot-covered stucco building on the central square. Hundreds of people were milling about. Buses and pick-up trucks with seats in the back waiting to leave for outlying areas were lined up down a side street. At 8 AM, there was much activity going on. A market was full of women moving about with plastic net bags full of vegetables and other produce, with young children tagging along or straddling their mothers in cloth slings across their backs. They crossed the street and walked a bit further down the square. A nameplate on a two-story office building announced the offices of the International Red Cross on the second floor.

"Red Cross, Efe. They would know about refugees and places for them in the area. Sure of it."

"Most probably. Let's ask."

"Hello, how can I help you?"

Stewart was the first to speak. He had noticed the man had a New Zealand accent. "My friend and I are looking to find a Lao refugee camp in the area. Someone we know may be working there and we are looking to join her."

"New Zealand, eh?" replied the Red Cross man who had identified himself as Derek.

"Yes, from Auckland. My friend's from Ghana. She believes her mother, who she has not seen for a long time, may be working at a center for refugees in the area. The village of Somdet Ya had been mentioned."

"Well, there is a camp at Somdet Ya. I know it well. We provide for a lot of its funding. Who are you looking for? There are not many non-Thai or non-Lao people at that place."

Efe piped up. She could not hold back any longer. "Her name is Jennifer Sutton. Do you recognize the name?"

"I certainly recognize it, Miss. I know her. I sent her there when she arrived in the area. Your mother is the best thing that has happened to that place in a long time. I can take you later. I have some things to attend to in the meantime. You can wait here or come back at 11."

"Wonderful. I cannot believe this is happening. It has been a long journey. My name is Efe Akala, by the way, and my friend is Stewart Bell. Thank you so much. We will be back at 11."

"Very good," said Derek. "You can leave your things here, behind the desk. They will be safe."

The 4-wheel drive entered the compound and stopped in front of a small building. Derek suggested they stay in the truck while he entered and saw if her mother was there. "Best if we do it this way. Need to make the meeting with your mother as private as possible. Lots of people around as you can see. Be back in a minute."

"Jenny, someone is here to see you." She was speaking to a group of girls in a meeting room at the back of the building.

"Oh, well, bring him in. I can see him in the office. I was expecting an official from the ministry."

"No, Jenny, it's more private than that."

"What's it about, Derek? Private?" replied Jenny with a frown.

"You'll see. I'll bring them in."

"Alright, in the office. Girls, we will have to postpone this discussion. Same time tomorrow." Private? Them? More than one person. What can this be about?

Efe Akala entered the room, followed by Stewart at a distance.

"Mommy, it's me, Efe."

Jenny was transfixed. Frozen. She stared at the young woman. A low slowly developing sob with tears forming in her eyes consumed her. She could not say anything. Did not, could not move. The moment seemed to last an eternity. What she had dreamed of, hoped for, despaired of, was happening. Not in Ghana, not in America, but here....in Thailand, in a camp far from her previous life. As she stared at her daughter, flashes ran through her mind - Efe as a baby, at three, at six, the last time she saw her, the pictures from the boarding school in Ghana. It was almost too much. She put her hands to her face, then took the three or four steps to embrace the lost daughter who had travelled halfway around the world to find her. They both cried, brought back their heads, looked at each other, then hugged again, with Jenny not letting go.

"My God, I can't believe this. How did you find me?" Before Efe could answer, Jenny continued. "How beautiful you are..... the most precious moment of my life," she said in a near whisper as she continued to gaze at her daughter, tears streaming down her face, oblivious to the presence of the others.

"How? Here? Efe? Why now? Where is Sisi? All this time. Everything I did to find you....... I was sure I would never see you again. The refusal at the school two years ago. Your father. What has happened?"

"Momma, we have so much to talk about. So much has happened. Daddy told me what happened. He was sorry. Told me everything the day before he died. It was not you. It was him....with Grandma.....being African. All so much. I understood, and I knew that I had to find you. You have many friends, Momma. I found them and because of them, I am here."

"He died. When? How? And where is Sisi?"

"Leukemia, six months ago, Momma. The night before he died, he made me promise to say to you he was sorry. And Sisi. She is back in Ghana."

"Oh, Efe. Efe. Efe." Jenny embraced her daughter once again, held her tight. It was then that Jenny noticed the young man standing a few paces away. "And who is this?"

"Bodyguard, Madam," replied the imposing fellow with the full head of blond hair. "Name is Stewart. I am a friend of your daughter from university back in England."

"England. You are in university in England, Efe? My God, we have so much to talk about," said Jenny

"I think I will leave you two alone," said Stewart.

"No, no, not necessary," said Jenny. "We need to find another place to go to. There are a lot of people around here. Not really the place for this......My God, what a surprise. I am overwhelmed..... I have a place in the village. Small house. We can go there. There is room for both of you, by the way. I have nothing else to do here today."

At that moment, Peggy Nash appeared in the doorway. "I think I know what this is about," she said with a huge smile as she observed the scene. "This is your daughter, isn't it, Jenny?"

"Yes, it is, Peggy. She just showed up here with Derek and her friend. She found me. I'm over the top. I don't know what else to say.......Efe, this is Peggy. It's her school.....who I work with."

Derek drove Jenny and Efe to the house in the village, then suggested to Stewart they go into Nong Khai for the rest of the day. Stewart accepted. "They need to be together. Thank you, sir. I will be a tourist today."

"I will bring you back this evening. And....we will eat in the village if the ladies want to do that. Little restaurant here that is very good. It will be on me," said Derek.

31

"How did you learn of it all, Efe? You said your father told you......before he died. You said it was leukemia."

"Yes, leukemia. It all came about very quickly. I had to rush home from Sheffield. I found a bundle of your letters to us, Momma, when we were little.... In father's things the day before he died. I asked him what really happened. He told me you just left. I then brought out the letters. He broke down. Told me everything."

"How did he explain it?" asked Jenny.

"He said he was sorry. That he loved you and still did. It was about him, being African and a Muslim, his own identity. He said he had lost it, that he was miserable at the time...with himself. I guess being with you made him feel less African and Muslim than American, that he was living a lie. So different from the rest of the family there. That, plus the pressure he was apparently under to protect the family's fortunes. Told me that after Grandpa died, Grandma forced him to accept taking Ankela as wife to solidify the family power in the region. He had kept knowledge of the pressure away from you, but Grandma never let up. She intercepted all the letters. Threw them away, then had the local mail office do it."

"I sent them every month for years, Efe."

"I know that now, Momma." Efe rose from the chair on the patio, went over to her mother and hugged her as they both stood. While in the embrace that lingered for a moment, Jenny asked "What about Sisi? Where is she? What is happening with her?"

"She's in Yendi. Finished high school in Accra in June. She is getting married."

"Married? She's still a child."

"Not really, any more, Momma, but she is too young for this. Grandma set it up......she will be marrying a young man from Tamale. Another political thing, I am sure. The family is losing influence - Uncle Kofi in Sheffield told me Grandma's cousin had been ousted from his long position as Minister of the Interior - and it looks like Grandma is up to re-arranging things once again. Sisi is going to go through with it. It is supposed to happen in January, after the fellow finishes some part of his military service in a UN mission somewhere. She doesn't want to go to university. She could if she wanted to. Daddy provided the money for that. I guess that money will go to a dowry. All being handled by Grandma. Sisi won't listen to me."

Efe paused a moment, then continued. "I must say that Sisi has always been pliant to Grandma's wishes. She was closer to Daddy than I was, as well. She was not present when Daddy told me what happened the day before he died. When I told her about it, she refused to believe it. The letters from you, the attempt to reach us in Accra at the school and what we were told, she did not want to believe any of it, not even hear about it."

"Is Grandma aware you have been looking for me?"

"Yes. Said she would disown me, cut off the funds for university. Threatened me. But, there was something she did not know. That Daddy had left me money. He knew."

"He knew what?" asked Jenny.

"That Grandma would try to control everything. I found out later he put aside even more money for us in an account in London that only I could sign for should he die."

"Momma, I guess Daddy understood that Grandma had ruined his life. He was not going to let it completely ruin mine and Sisi's....for Sisi, provided she did not want it to be that way. Grandma did not know what to say when I told her about the money in the London bank. Silence at the end of the line. She actually had Uncle Kofi throw me out of the house in Sheffield. I went to stay with my friend Kate and her parents until I left for here. I think it will be difficult with Sisi. Grandma will not want the same thing to happen with her. The marriage and all of that. She needs that to happen."

"Efe, do you want to return to Ghana?"

"No. There is nothing for me there. Only betrayal. I want to be with you."

Jenny and her daughter spent the next two days re-living as much as they could the lives of each other that they had missed.

Stewart Bell could see his part of the arrangement with Efe had been fulfilled. He decided to move on, visit as much as he could of the rest of Thailand, before returning to Sheffield. "Efe, I'm going to Chiang Mai. A trip on an elephant is awaiting me. A lot of them there, apparently. You don't need me anymore. I have my return ticket to the U.K. I'm going to bum around for awhile. Plenty to see. You found your Mum. That's the important thing. I will be fine."

"Stewie, you were great. A true friend. I will always be grateful."

"Well, I'll see you back at university."

"I don't know. I may not be going back to Sheffield. I may be going to the States with my mum or stay here with her for awhile. We're not separating again. No way."

"I can understand. But I hope to see you again. Kate and the others will miss you if you don't come back."

"Friends are friends, Stewie. I will never be far. Thanks again."

Peggy, Jenny and Efe were having lunch at the little outdoor restaurant two days later. Peggy spoke first. "Jenny, you and Efe have to get out of here. Move on. This has changed everything for you. You don't have to stay here. I can manage. Go back to the States. Like I said, move on."

"Peggy, dear, you have been a wonderful friend. I would love to stay and continue the work You have given me peace, something meaningful for me to do. I am torn. We are on the way to getting the funding you need to make all this worthwhile. I just can't leave you like that."

"I can manage, Jen. Derek is staying. He has extended his assignment in Nong Khai. The funding will go through..... What is Efe going to do? Follow us around here and miss out on finishing university? Interrupting that would be foolish. The reason you came here was to escape from what you had lost. You have found what you had lost, my dear, at least part of it anyway. There is no reason for you to stay. Git! Go home! I'm serious," said Peggy in her slow Oklahoma drawl.

Jenny and Efe arrived in New York later in August. They had made a stop in the U.K. for Efe to recover her things at the Wilsons and tell the university she would be transferring to a university in the United States. They also spent an evening with an overjoyed Margaret Bishop and an aging Buckeye in Ealing. On the way to their hotel, Efe saw a florist shop that was open, asked the taxi driver to stop, went in and came out with a yellow rose that she gave her mother. "A promise to Daddy, Mom.... He insisted I do this if I found you. What does the gift of a yellow rose mean to someone?"

"For some, Efe, it means 'I care'. For others, it means 'Remember me'." Jenny had tears in her eyes as she looked out the window.

Between their arrival and the end of September when Jenny could re-occupy her apartment in New York, the two of them stayed in Connecticut with her sister Margie's husband and his second wife who Jenny had always liked. The first week of September was spent in Well's Beach, Maine at the beachfront house Jenny had rented on numerous occasions in the past. Her sister Molly and most of her nieces and nephews joined them there for the long Labor Day weekend. The reunion was joyous for all. Efe had been a distant thought for all of them since they were little. Here she was, a beautiful, smart and fun girl who was clearly overjoyed with finding the American side of her family. Days on the beach, an evening on the pier and the amusement park at Old Orchard, clams at Joe's clam shack in Ogunquit. Happy times. Something was missing for Jenny, though, and that was Sisi. Back in Ghana. Engaged to be married. No interest in her mother. Still so far away.

One evening, Efe told her mother that she had an idea.

"Mom, I have a friend in Accra who speaks with Sisi regularly; at least she did when we were at school. I am going to call her tomorrow. This is crazy for Sisi. Getting married. Will be stuck back there. I can't believe she will be happy. She apparently hardly knows the man. The last time I spoke with her when she said she wanted nothing to do with you, she told me she was looking forward to being the wife of a military officer who had political connections. He would be influential and she would continue to have a privileged life. This all comes from Grandma, of course. But Sisi has never been outside the country. Not like me. I saw so many aspects of life outside of our little world. Sisi has experienced none of that. I want her to know the other side. Daddy is gone. Grandma is getting old and does not have Sisi's best interests at heart to begin with. She has little to stay there for."

"I am at a loss of what to do, Efe. We could go there and try to convince her to leave. I can't trust the government, though. They could somehow try to detain you in the country, although that would probably have to come from Grandma and you say she has less influence now," Jenny said.

"I am going to ask my friend if she could be a go-between, without alerting Grandma. We will see where this can take us," said Efe.

Mustafa Korafa recognized the voice. "Korafa, I have something for you" said the Russian. "There is telephone traffic we have picked up you may be interested in. Between a young woman in Accra and the phone of the woman in Yendi your associate Kuma has been watching. Calls with the woman's granddaughter, talking about going to America."

"What is being said?" replied Korafa.

"We have recorded three phone calls to Yendi from this young lady. There were two phone calls from New York to her that we picked up as well. All connected, it seems. I can give you a tape of the recordings. I am offering this to you, Korafa, out of continuing appreciation for your services over the years. Tell me, what do you want us to do with this?"

"We must meet. The cafe on the road outside Accra. Usual place. When can you do it?"

"Thursday, 8 PM, two days from now." replied the Russian.

"See you there."

"I can't leave and go to America," Sisi Akala told her friend. "I am to be married here in January. It's not possible. I don't know what Efe is doing with this. Our mother abandoned us when we were little."

"Sisi, I have spoken to Efe twice now. She really wants to talk to you. Why can't you do it? You could call from here when you are in Accra. She is in New York, with your mother. She seems very happy about being there."

"I can't do this. I am getting married in four months. Efe is trying to convince me to leave it all. I won't."

"Sisi, I think you should speak with her. You may get a different picture in your mind. Ghana is not America."

"Bina, I don't know America. I know Ghana. I have never even been outside the country since coming here as a child."

"It's your sister. You should talk to her."

"OK. I will. I will be in Accra next Wednesday at my cousin's place. I will go to your house in the evening."

"Sisi, I found Momma as you are aware by now. It is not what you think. I am not going back to Ghana, nor back to university in England. I will go to university here. Our mother has been wonderful, Sisi. She is not what you think, what you have always been told." Sisi did not say anything. She was listening. Efe continued, "We want you to come to New York. You can come here for a visit and see for yourself what it is like, what life with our mother could be. Sisi, don't do this marriage thing so fast. You are not even eighteen yet. You hardly know the man."

"I can't, Efe. I have promised to do it. My life is here. I know nothing of America," said Sisi.

There was a momentary break in the conversation. A new voice came on the line. "Sisi, this is your mother. I love you, my dear. I have always loved you. I never abandoned you. I just want to see you."

Sisi remembered the voice. It came back to her. The tall lady so high above her, bending over to kiss her on the forehead, as she sat on the floor of the old whitewashed house in Yendi. Silence. A few seconds passed. "I don't know what to say.....Mother. I hardly remember you. Why is this so difficult?"

"Sisi, please come here. I want to see you. You can decide what to do after that. Can we talk about doing it? I have so much to tell you and so much to learn from you about your life and what you have done all these years. I love you, Sisi. I always have."

"Maybe, maybe, Momma." replied the young girl on the phone who was beginning to cry.

"Sisi, you can come here for a week or two. I will send you the money.....We can speak again. We can talk about all this. Call us here. Here is the number. Bina can do it for you," said Jenny, trying to find a way to make sure another connection would be made.

"I will think about it. Goodbye."

Bina looked at Sisi as her friend replaced the receiver. "Well, you should think about it. You don't have to drop getting married. Your mother is talking about you going for a visit. You can see then. You don't have to disrupt everything."

"Maybe. Maybe. I have to leave. Thank you, Bina."

"When will you come back? What are you going to do?"

"I don't know. I will call you."

Sisi took the bus back to Accra the following Tuesday, telling her grandmother she wanted to see her cousin again. She spent an hour walking around the center of the city, not sure of what she was about to unleash. Bina opened the door to see Sisi blurting out before saying hello, "Can you see if they are at the number in New York?"

"It is actually in Connecticut. I will try it. Come in."

The phone rang a few times and then a message kicked in. Bina realized the time there was 10:30 in the morning. She left a message for Efe to call her in Accra.

"Sisi, it's me, Efe, with Momma. Do you want to speak with me or with her?"

"Give her to me." Sisi wasted no time in telling her mother she was accepting what had been proposed.

"Yes, yes, Sisi. I am so happy you want to do this.......when can you come?"

"As soon as I can. It is September now. A good time. I have to get a passport.....I thought a lot about it. I want to do it. I will then see about the rest."

"This is wonderful. I am so happy. Your sister wants to speak to you."

"Sisi, this is great you are doing this. Good for you, good for all of us. Makes me happy. Tell us when you are coming. Momma will have to send you the money for the ticket."

"I will. I will let Bina know so she can call you. Bye." Sisi knew that her grandmother would not be happy with this.

"You are what? Going for a visit to America? No, you are not. I won't allow it. You are getting married in a few weeks. You can't be going off on trips like that. Efe and your mother are deceiving you. They will just convince you to stay, to not return to your chosen life here. You will humiliate the family of the man you are supposed to be marrying. Humiliate our family. Your place is here, Sisi. I won't allow it. I will not sign for your passport. Without my permission, you cannot get it. No. You are not going to do this."

Sisi had not thought of that. She had not known that, still being under eighteen, she would require the signature of a parent or guardian on the passport application. "Grandmama, I want to do this. I have to see what Efe has seen. There is not much of our family that remains here, by the way. But I will come back. I intend to go through with the marriage. I have not changed my mind on that. You must not believe that I have. Please, let me do this. I must see my mother. I have thought about it. It has been too long."

"No, Sisi. I will not allow it. You will not have your passport, at least not now, before you are married. You will be eighteen three days after your marriage in January. You can get a passport all by yourself then, I will not be able to stop you, but you will by then be married. Stop this foolishness. Your mother just wants to kidnap you, take you away from your roots here. You are African, not American."

Bina called Efe and Jenny to tell them about the situation. Sisi could not get a passport by herself. Furthermore, she was being grounded in Yendi. "I'm sorry, Efe. I have done what I could. Your grandmother here is making things very difficult for her."

Bina Okura recognized the young man dressed in army fatigues as he entered the cafe. He was a cousin who she knew had recently been with Ghana's peacekeeping forces somewhere in Africa. "Hey, Ollie, over here. Come over.........How are you?" The young man turned, recognized Bina and came over to the table.

"Bina.... Good to see you. How is your father?"

"My father....and my mother. are well. Both still working for the government. And you? Military service? I never would have thought."

"Military service has been OK. As you can see, I am an officer, a lieutenant, so far at least. I enlisted after high school and was invited a few months later to go to officer training. I just spent a year in Namibia, helping police things there."

"Ollie, do you remember Efe Akala and her younger sister, Sisi? They were at St. Francis with me."

"Yes. Efe the tall one, beautiful and smart. So was her little sister, as I remember, but a shy girl. Not like Efe," said Ollie.

"Well, Efe is in America. Went searching for her mother who was American and had not seen or heard from her since she was a child. She found her somewhere in Asia. Quite a story. And Sisi. She is marrying in a few months, to an army officer. I bring it up because I thought you may know him. He has been in peacekeeping as well."

"The younger girl, Sisi, is pretty young, isn't she? Getting married? What is the man's name?"

"Kwame Elbah."

Ollie looked at Bina, dropped his head and moved closer to her. Glancing to one side, then the other, he said almost in a whisper, "Kwame Elbah, Lieutenant Kwame Elbah, has AIDS, Bina. He should not be marrying anyone. He spent two months in hospital in Namibia, supposedly with pneumonia. It's AIDS. I know. Our medical officer told me. Officers higher up have kept it under wraps. His family is influential..... Does Sisi know this? She should not be marrying this guy. No one should be marrying him. It is a death sentence. I don't care what many people here say about the disease. It doesn't go away. It kills."

"My God." Bina brought her hands to her face and looked despairingly at the young man.

"Bina, Sisi Akala has to be told this. She cannot marry this man."

"If she came here, Ollie, would you tell her what you told me?"

"I can't be identified with this. Not so easily anyway. Not in person. Perhaps by telephone I could. She has to be made aware of this. She can't go through with it." He paused before continuing, "But my identity must not be known. Bina, you will have to tell her. If she does not believe you or insists on hearing it from your source, then perhaps we could have a telephone call. I hope it doesn't have to come to that, but if it does, I would have to make sure it is not overheard by anyone else and my identity not divulged. I could be in trouble if it did. I wish it were otherwise. The attitude of the military about AIDS and what to do about it is very worrisome. Denial at all levels."

"OK, I will have to tell her, Ollie." Bina stopped herself before telling him about Sisi's plan to see her mother. Sensitive stuff. The Agyas still had influence in the country.

The phone rang in Yendi. Sisi answered. "Sisi, this is Bina. Are you alone?"

"No. Why? My grandmother is somewhere in the house. What is it?"

"Call me when you are alone. I have something important to tell you."

"OK. It may be today or even tomorrow. Wait....I will call from the post office telephone tomorrow. I will tell Mama I am going to fetch the mail."

Sisi phoned the following morning. "Bina, what is it? What do you need to tell me?"

"Your fiancé has AIDS, Sisi. You can't be marrying him."

"What? AIDS? That is about homosexuals. My future husband is a homosexual? What are you telling me?"

"Sisi, listen, AIDS is not just about homosexuals. People get it by having sex with others who already have it. It's not just about gay people. Men and women. Someone who knows your fiancé told me all this. I cannot tell you who. But it's real. I have full confidence in my source. You must not marry this man, Sisi. It will be a death sentence. There is no cure for AIDS."

"How would he have gotten it, Bina?"

"Sisi, don't be so naive. Peacekeeping. Another country. Away from home. Sex with someone, for God's sake. Over there or maybe here. There is AIDS in Ghana."

"I don't believe this, Bina. My family would not allow this to happen. My grandmother. She would be told this."

"Would she? I am not so sure. Honor of the man's family. Denial, Sisi. The alternative is humiliation. People in this country are in denial about AIDS. Fortunately, my parents are in the government and know something about it, enough about the dangers of it and the general refusal of the leaders of the country to do something or even to speak of its danger."

"How can I know this for sure? Can I speak with the person who told you?" asked Sisi.

"Yes, if you wish, but he cannot be identified. It is very sensitive. But he is willing to tell you over the telephone what he told me. He will just not give you his name. He does not want people dying because of his silence. He just has to be careful."

"When can I speak with him? I must hear it from him."

"Saturday. He could come to our house. You could call us from the post office. My parents are always out on Saturday mornings. Saturday morning at 10 o'clock. Could we try for that?"

"I will need to get away from Mama. But, yes, Saturday morning at 10 o'clock. I will call you."

"Grandmama, I must tell you something very grave. I am not going to marry Kwame. I do not want to die young. Kwame has AIDS. I cannot marry him."

"You what? You are telling me what? The man you are going to marry has this AIDS? What? Who told you this?"

"A man who knows him, Mama. I spoke with him. I believe him. I can't marry Kwame. I do not want to get this disease."

"Sisi, what you may believe about this disease is all wrong. It is a disease of gay people. And Kwame is not gay. His family. Not possible. It is not true what you have been told. Who told you this?"

"I don't have his name, so I can't tell you who it is. Mama, Kwame was in a hospital in Namibia for two months. He never told me about that. Did you know of it?"

"No, nothing of him being sick or in a hospital. This is foolish. You have nothing to worry about. You will be married and you will see, everything will be fine."

"Mama, I don't want the disease. I found some documentation on it at the Oxfam center. I will not do it."

"Sisi, I am your guardian and you will listen to me. Stop this foolishness."

"Will you tell Kwame's family about what I have told you? Will you ask them about this? They should know."

"I will not discuss this with them. It is trash talk you are playing around with. AIDS is only with people who are homosexuals and Kwame is not. I won't have you spreading this around, either."

"I am not going to go through with the marriage, Mama. I won't do it."

"Yes, you will. You have three months to prepare. You will not humiliate our family with your foolishness."

Three days later, Grandmama Akala met the former intelligence officer at the cafe outside of Yendi. "I want you to observe everything my granddaughter does. You will be announced as the new caretaker of the compound. If she leaves the house, follow her. Everywhere. Use whatever resources you need. I need to know who she speaks to, what telephone calls are made and from where. She is not to know she is being followed. You are supposed to be good at this. Can I rely on you?"

"Yes, Madame, you may rely on me." Wilson Kuma left the cafe and got into his vehicle. This will make things easier, he thought as he got onto the road going south. The President's people will like this.

Two days later, Kuma was on the phone with the President's deputy chief of staff. "This is very good, Kuma. We have little proof of the murders. We know a lot about the payoffs, but nothing about the circumstances of the disappearances. We need something on those to carry out our operation against the family. They were behind them. We are certain of that. You will be inside the home there. Maybe somebody will make a mistake. Keep me informed."

"Yes, sir," replied Kuma. "You can count on it. I need a secure telephone, however. These calls on regular lines especially from places like Yendi are risky. Can you get me a secure cellular phone?"

"I will see what I can do. Call me Thursday, two days from now."

Bina placed the call to Connecticut. "Efe, the man Sisi is to marry has AIDS. I learned of it a week ago, from someone I have known for a long time, but whose identity must remain secret. I have no reason to doubt what he said and I informed Sisi of it. Since the discussion with her, I have not been able to reach her. The number in Yendi has been changed. She probably told your grandmother about what I said and as a result communications have been cut."

"AIDS? Oh, my God. I can't believe my grandmother would force her to do this if she knew what AIDS was really about."

"Efe, people here in Ghana are ignorant about it. They don't appreciate what it is and how it is killing people. My parents work in the government and grasp all of that. If Sisi marries this man, it will be a death sentence."

"Listen, Bina. My mother is not here right now. Can we call you back?"

"Sure. I'm sorry to have to tell you this."

Later that afternoon

"Momma, we will have to go get Sisi."

"My God. AIDS. My baby......" Jenny was stunned, but quickly looked at Efe and replied. "Yes, we will have to go get her."

32

Jenny phoned Tim, who in turn rang Brian in Paris and Jay in New York. He set up a conference call from his office in Boston. "Guys, we need to mount an operation to get Jenny's other daughter out of Ghana. The grandmother has her locked down; she is scheduled to be married in January to a guy who has AIDS, for God's sake, and all communications have been cut off. We have 90 days to organize something or the girl is married and gets the first shot of the plague."

Tim heard soft 'Ohhs' from both Peterson and Maxwell as he finished. Brian was the first to say something. "The girl can't get away from the house? She's going to be locked up for three months? If we got her money with a plane ticket somehow, could she not escape with some help from people in the country and fly out to Paris or New York?"

"She's not eighteen yet, Brian. She can't get a passport. She is in that northern town far away from Accra. Her grandmother is her guardian and is withholding any permission for her to get a passport and undoubtedly has someone looking over everything the girl does. Jenny's contact in Accra says the fiancé's family is influential and the grandmother wants the marriage to happen at all costs."

"At the risk of her granddaughter surely contracting AIDS and dying?" asked Brian.

"Brian, you know as well as I do many Africans don't believe the stuff about AIDS. Big time denial. They don't want to believe any of it. The grandmother is probably no different. In any case, Jenny, her daughter Efe and their contact in Accra say that Grandma needs this marriage to save the family's fortune and influence."

Jay Peterson knew something about that. "Guys, I have had some digging done in Accra on the Akala and Agya families. Jenny's mother-in-law is an Agya. You will remember that her cousin was the Minister of the Interior for a long time. Got suspended from that a few months ago by the President, then got reinstated somehow. The President found out the man was taking bribes big time from resource companies and keeping the money for himself. Also suspected the man had a young and promising politician murdered. Someone in the President's orbit. But, like I said, he got reinstated. Made some sort of amends with the old man. Grandma must be nervous. She is the matriarch."

Tim put forth his idea. "I worked for a while in northwest Mali years ago and made some friends there. One of them is a very resourceful guy who took Jenny undetected into northern Ghana four years or so ago to extract the girls. They did not succeed in getting to them, but they found out where they were, at least. Travelled halfway through Ghana without being detected. I think you probably heard of it one way or the other from Jenny. Anyway, the guy knows the route to get in and out, knows Yendi as well from the time he and Jenny were there. Jenny trusts him. He's good, former paratrooper, speaks Akan as well....... My idea is to capture the girl, bring her across the border through the bush, through Burkina, then Mali and into Dakar, then here. Overland route from Yendi to Dakar, maybe use the railroad from Kayes to Dakar for the last leg. Avoid airports as much as we can. I was told years ago that Ghanaian intelligence has tentacles everywhere on the continent as do most of the other African countries as well, most probably with IOUs and favors to be collected. We can't afford to be exposed to big eyes and ears at airports."

"OK," responded Brian. "What do you need from me? Jay, I don't know you very well. We never really met, but Tim has told me a lot. I guess you know the whole story. From what you say, you have managed to follow a bit of the intrigues over there."

Jay responded. "I will share all that I know and given what you are telling me, Tim, I will get back with my contacts in the region."

"Brian, in response to your question about what you could do, you are welcome to be part of the extraction team," said Tim. "You know Africa even better than I do. We may not need for you to actually be with us in Ghana, though. We will be three in a Land Rover going in and four coming out as it is. We certainly will need to alert the U.S. authorities in Bamako, Ouagadougou and Dakar about what we are doing. The girl will need papers to be able to leave Senegal, perhaps even transit Mali. Same thing for Burkina Faso. She is an American citizen but most probably does not know where any of those papers are that would substantiate such. Could you look after that stuff?"

"I have been working with the State Department long enough. I think I could get them to cooperate."

Tim interceded. "Jenny tells me there is someone in Washington at State who could help. A Susan Riley. Helped her a couple of years ago to get messages to her daughters in Accra. Got through all of the BS that was in the files about her. Jenny thinks she would be willing to intercede for whatever is needed from there. We are already on to getting the girl's birth certificate from Ohio."

Brian asked the question. "What are the risks?"

"That we get caught. In Ghana. We will need some help on the inside if we do. We will be contacting Seydou Touré, our Malian friend as soon as we can. He will be key to all this. He said to Jenny the first time around that he had a powerful friend who owes him one. But, in the end, only one of us needs to be on the Ghana phase of the operation. Ideally, it would be Seydou and I with Jenny, who insists on being part of the operation. She wants to be the one to tell her daughter they have come for her. She's a tough lady. We will have to figure the best time for this - can't let it ride too long. Anything could happen to the girl."

"Jay, are you OK with the intelligence part of it? I don't think you need to be with us over there. Up to you."

"I don't need to be there, but maybe I will be in Dakar. I know somebody there who could help. By the way, you don't want to use the railroad. All sorts of people on those trains. Avoid it. Go by car. A long drive into Dakar, but safer."

Jay asked Tim the question. "Aren't you taking a pretty serious personal risk going into Ghana this way?"

"Jay, I've been working in this development business for years now. This is a chance to do something really important for someone that is critical to her life. I've seen a lot. So have you. Africa, Asia. I helped a young woman once; got her out of her own hell and saved her life. I think I can do it again. I don't have a family, in any case. I don't need to worry about that sort of stuff. This lady is so close to having her family back. Need to close the deal. I'm into it. We will get it done."

Tim called Jenny and explained the plan. She was relieved. She then placed the call to Seydou's nephew in Bamako. She told him of her need to speak with his uncle as soon as possible. Two days later, Seydou reached Jenny. He was in. He said the trip would have to be when there is no moon. Tim and Jenny phoned back the following day and fleshed out the key details. Seydou suggested the moonless nights of the third week of October, assuming they could get Sisi's passport from Washington by that time. They could not afford to put it off another month. A photograph would be needed. Jenny took the picture she was given in Jirapa to a photoshop and soon had a headshot of Sisi that would have to do. She sent it by courier to Susan Riley, who called two days later and said the photo would be fine. It could take two weeks. "But it will be done," she assured Jenny.

"Nobody must know we are doing this outside of us," said Tim as he, Jenny, Jay and Efe met. "Many US officials are aware of it. We had little choice. State in D.C. knows about it. Cannot afford to have problems at the borders. Already a lot of people are in the loop; can't let this get any wider. Except Bina. She should know and make sure Sisi stays in Yendi the third week of October. And Seydou's contact in Ghana. He says it will be fine. Let's hope so."

The next morning Jenny phoned Bina "Bina, we are coming to Ghana to get Sisi. To Yendi. It will be the third week of October, three weeks from now. I can't tell you more. Sisi of course must be in Yendi at that time. You have told us she has been grounded. She has to be there for this to work. If Sisi contacts you, do not say anything about it, but please, please find out from her if she has any plans to be elsewhere during that week. If she for some reason is to be elsewhere, we have to know. We will postpone the operation to when we can count on her being there. Can you help us with that, Bina?"

"Yes, Madame. I will. I don't think she will be contacting me, however. It appears that she has been truly grounded. I called her a few days ago, but a man answered and said she was not available. I left him a request for her to call me, but I never got anything back."

Jenny turned to Efe after hanging up. "Could she be elsewhere? Could they have taken her somewhere else? There is no way for us to know. I hope this doesn't turn out to be a wild goose chase."

"A wild goose chase, Momma?"

"Ohio, Efe. Ohio. Sayings from home. You will hear more," Jenny said as she smiled at her daughter.

"Now, to get you enrolled somewhere. No word back from the universities here....We will have to follow up on that. There is Sisi and then there is you. Have to get you going here," said Jenny.

"Momma, I have no idea how good these universities are. I am relying totally on you."

"Don't worry. They're good. And expensive. But your grandfather Sutton's trust fund for us, for you, as well as the money that you told me is in a bank in London for you will come in handy. They are top-notch universities and you will get a great education."

Sometime the next day

"Korafa, we have something for you. You can get it when you come to Accra," said the Russian.

Three days later, Mustafa Korafa turned off the tape recorder. So, she is coming here. How interesting. I will do this myself. Kuma is guarding the girl but he is working for the boss. I will do this myself.

33

Jenny and Tim arrived in Paris the morning of that October day and connected with Brian before taking an afternoon flight to Bamako. The three of them had spoken two days before. Jenny confirmed that she had received Sisi's temporary passport from Susan Riley's office in D.C. Susan had also told Jenny that the U.S. people in Bamako, Ouagadougou, Accra and Dakar were informed of what would be happening. If called upon to facilitate the entry or exit of them into or out of any of the four countries, they would cooperate and do what needed to be done. Jenny was told it was unusual, but given what the State Department now knew about the Sutton-Akala file, they would cooperate.

"Here we go," said Brian as the plane touched off. "Operation Recovery of Your Life Phase Two, Jenny."

"You know, Brian, I remember very well the first time we met. You promised me what I told you would stay with you. It didn't but I'm glad it didn't. Tim and Jay would not have known about this and I could very well have no chance of doing what we are doing. I was really upset with you for spilling my story. But I forgive you," said Jenny.

"You deserved assistance. I couldn't do much on my own. You needed help. Couldn't keep it to myself. Hey, we are on the way to closing the deal."

"Yep, closing the deal."

"By the way, how is your oldest acclimatizing to America?" asked Brian. "Big change."

"She is doing just fine. Coming to find me in Thailand was something. She is a smart and tough girl. My husband may have been a real shit for me, but he did a good job with her. Intelligent, considerate, good manners. What do I say? She has connected with her various cousins back home and is on the way to being accepted in one of the universities in Boston. One of her cousins took her to a Bruce Springsteen concert the other night. She's loving it."

"What was behind your husband doing this?"

"His own self-identity, apparently, Brian. And......Africa. The pressures of being African. He told Efe he did wrong, was sorry he did what he did, actually loved me to the end. It's sad."

It had been agreed with Seydou Touré that he would meet them at the hotel later that evening. "Too many eyes and ears at the airport," he said, cognizant of the clandestine activities of the various governments of Africa that always wanted to know who was coming in. People could follow the party to the hotel and perhaps surmise that something was afoot, but having the former paratrooper meet the trio at the airport with a beat up old Land Rover would certainly attract attention. Jenny, Tim and Brian were dressed as businesspeople and told the border officials they were in Mali to discuss a business deal in the capital and then travel to Ouagadougou for a tourist visit before returning to New York. As a precaution, Seydou had parked in the lane opposite the exit from the airport and followed the taxi to the hotel, observing if any other vehicle was following them. There were none that he could detect.

Soon after arriving at the hotel, Jenny phoned Bina in Accra. "Bina, this is Efe's mother. I can't tell you where I am right now, but do you know if Sisi is in Yendi?"

"No, I don't, but she was there two days ago. She tried to reach me, apparently. Spoke with my mother. She was crying, then had to hang up. Are you coming to get her? Are you on your way?"

"Yes, we are and I have to leave. If Sisi calls you, just suggest to her that she stay where she is. Say it will be best for her. Please say nothing more. Her telephone may be bugged."

Later that evening, Jenny, Tim and Brian walked the short distance from the hotel to the Land Rover parked down the road. Before getting to it, Tim turned around to make sure no one was observing or following them. The evening was quiet. No one was around. They proceeded to Seydou's nephew's home for a meal and final discussion of the plan. Seydou and Jenny also managed to exchange what had happened to them in the intervening four plus years since their initial foray into Ghana.

Tim asked Seydou about his own life.

"*Eh bien.* Nioro du Sahel is a boring place, as you know, Tim, but I found a new business. The Canadian project was expanded, more Canadians came to the town as well as a large group of Frenchmen for a project of their own. They needed fresh vegetables so I started a garden with my wife. Within a year we were supplying all the needs of the Canadians and the French, who are not as nice as the Canadians by the way, for their tomatoes and lettuce. Soon, with seeds from Canada, we were also producing cucumbers, radishes, and carrots. My wife is now in charge. We have fifteen women working in the garden. Friends of mine told me I was so prosperous now, I could take a second wife. I told them that I was not interested in doing that. I knew too much about the problems," chuckled Seydou as he looked mischievously at Jenny and the others.

"You better not take a second wife, Seydou Touré, or I will bop you one real good," said Jenny.

"What is 'bop'? I don't know that word," asked Seydou.

"Take a big iron frying pan like the one over there and hit you over the head," said Jenny.

"*Vous avez un côté méchant, Madame.* You have a mean side to you," said the African with a laugh. After a pause, Seydou continued. "Back to our task. One thing we have not established yet. How will we get your daughter out of the house?"

"I have an idea," said Jenny who proceeded to outline what she had in mind.

"Oh, who is he, Seydou? Your friend in Ghana," asked Tim.

"Deputy head of the national police force. No need to say his name. His people patrol the border amongst other things. I was taking a chance, but I trust him. We will have to know who to turn to if we have a problem."

"What did you tell him?" asked Tim.

"That I would be helping a young lady reunite with her mother after the death of her father. The young lady was being held against her wishes by her grandmother who was very nasty. I asked him not to continue with questions. He said that he trusted me, that he owed me a big favor and if helping out in this took care of the favor, he would do what he could, just as long as it was not about betraying his country. I told him he would not be doing any of that," replied Seydou.

Later that morning, they crossed into Burkina Faso without incident. Before dark, after going around Ouagadougou and travelling south toward Ghana, Seydou went off road. He took the same route he had taken four years before to avoid the checkpoints. Around 10 PM on a pitch dark night, they crossed what he believed to be the line of the border and went seven or eight kilometers into Ghana to camp for the night. They had not been followed. Seydou had to be careful. With no lights, the going was very slow to avoid hitting holes, gullies, trees or even animals. It was still the rainy season as well, with the possibility of a rushing stream filling a normally dry riverbed. They crossed two streams that had water without incident. On more than one occasion, they heard the clanging of bells of either goats or cattle who were in movement nearby. They could not afford to hit a cow or a goat and cause trouble with a herder.

So, they have landed in Bamako, and crossed into Burkina. Tourist visas, the man said. One white man. Canadian. The same Canadian who was in Accra. A Malian. Military man, they say. And Jenny. Well, Jenny, it will soon be what you Americans call pay-back time. Mustafa Korafa knew everything they were doing. The Russians are everywhere. Rather the men who work for the Russians are everywhere, thought Korafa as he put the phone down and prepared to drive to Yendi. It will take them the day to cross Burkina. They can only be in Yendi tomorrow. I will be waiting for them. He packed some gear into his Toyota jeep and left.

The Land Rover was parked above the Akala compound. Seydou had the binoculars while Jenny and Tim kept their heads down in the back.

"What do you see?" she asked.

"Two vehicles, a Rover like this one, only newer, and a small Toyota pick-up truck. No signage on either vehicle. Ah......a tall man has crossed the yard to the building in the back," replied Seydou.

"Let me see. Tall man? Who could that be?" said Jenny

She took the binoculars but the man had entered the far building that she remembered as the vet clinic. There did not appear to be any animals around. "Looks like no more veterinary practice here," she said. A minute later, a man emerged from the building and walked back to the house. "Don't recognize him. Have no idea who he could be," she said as she lowered the binoculars.

"We cannot wait here much longer, Madame. We will be noticed. We have to decide what to do," said Seydou.

Tim spoke up. "We have to find out if your daughter is in the house. I have an idea. Seydou, you stay here on foot. There are some bushes over there. Looks like you may be able to hide yourself in them. Just lay down and watch the house. I will take the vehicle with Jenny, find a place to stay put for a couple hours, then come back here to get you, learn what you have seen. If you are observed, walk down the hill to the outdoor restaurant down there and wait for us. If you are not up here, we will know where you are. Jenny, in the meantime, you have to lie down in the back and not be seen as we move around."

"Very good," said Seydou. "If somehow I get stopped, I will call my contact in Accra. In the meantime, though, we have to find out where your daughter is."

They found Seydou at the cafe down the hill two hours later. He rose from a table, left some money on it for his Coke and got into the vehicle. "She is there. Light skinned, tall like you, Madame. I saw her face. Definitely your daughter."

"OK, now my own little plan for getting her out of the house," said Jenny.

"Where is this man's house, Madame? We should go there now. We cannot afford to spend too much time riding around. We should try to get her out this evening."

"I have to speak to him. I believe he will help. He hated my mother-in-law, thought she was what killed his good friend, her husband. Thought she drove him to stress and cancer. I spoke to him six months after being thrown out of the house. He said if ever I needed a hand, he would be glad to help. He did tell me at that time that he could not intercede with my husband, though. If there was anything else I needed, he said he would help. He said he liked me and thought I was the best thing that happened to his friend's son. Was sorry to see the breakup. But things have changed. The men in the Akala family are gone. I am fairly certain he would love to get back at Madame Akala. Let's go. He lives not far from here."

"Isaac, how are you? It's Jenny."

Isaac Anang was very much surprised. He had difficulty saying anything for a moment. Finally, as he looked at the tall woman in the doorway, the old man blurted out "For the love of God, Jennifer, what a surprise. What brings you here? I have not seen you since you left Yendi. What? Fifteen years ago?"

"I need your help. Can I come in?"

"Yes, certainly. My wife died some years ago. My daughter and her husband live with me. They are not here just now. But please, come in."

Jenny sat down on the long cushioned sofa in the center of the room.

"This is horrible what you are telling me. But I can believe it. That woman is evil. The poor girl needs to be with her mother and sister. She has no one left here. The only reason the old woman is keeping her here is for her own benefit. The young man she is to marry is probably from some important family somewhere. And this AIDS. I believe you. My daughter has spoken to me of it......when do you want to do this?"

"Tonight. The longer we are here, the more chance we have of being detected. Madame is still a powerful person."

"Not so much anymore, I am told," replied Isaac. "But yes, you are right. As soon as possible. Here is what I propose. It will have to be tomorrow, though. My daughter has told me she often sees your daughter at a cafe not far from the Akala house accompanied by a bodyguard. I can ask Lizbeth if she could carry a note to her that will tell her to come somewhere later. That you are here. Slip it to her quickly when the bodyguard is not looking. There are many people who go there. She could be told to come here at midnight when no one else is awake. Lizbeth would take back the note so no one would find her with it. She could even tell Sisi verbally all of this if the bodyguard was not so close by. We could try it."

"All right. Your daughter will be willing to do that?" asked Jenny.

"She hates that Akala woman. Madame Akala made sure Lizbeth lost her job with the Transportation department five years ago. I think she will be open to doing something like this."

At that moment, Lizbeth Anang walked in the door. "My God, Jennifer Akala. What a surprise. I haven't seen you in years. What brings you here?"

Isaac Anang spoke first. "Her daughter. She is here to get her daughter."

Fifteen minutes later

"Of course I will do it. I will do whatever it takes to get that poor girl out of the clutches of that woman. What can she do to us now? She has no power anymore."

Mustafa Korafa had arrived in Yendi that afternoon. He was unsure where to go. He could not go to the Akala house. He would be unwelcome and he did not want Wilson Kuma to know he was around. He had to find the American woman and her colleagues some other way.

Jenny, Tim and Seydou ended up staying the night in the Anang house. Isaac insisted on it. The Land Rover was hidden behind the house. Someone would have to walk around the side of the house to see it. The yard in the back was protected by an eight foot wall on three sides. It would be difficult to make out the vehicle from any angle.

Jenny and Lizbeth spent a good part of the evening talking about their lives, often coming back to the topic of the condition of women in Africa. Lizbeth had been educated in a Catholic school in Tamale and had been a civil servant for fifteen years before being terminated through the influence of Madame Akala. She was a volunteer for a women's shelter that had been started in Yendi three years previously. "Madame Akala tried to have it shut down. Said to everyone in the town that women don't need protection. They just have to obey their husbands and everything will be all right. The Muslims don't think like us. It is very different for them, as you know. But the local governor who had been elected that year said no, the center would go forward. Needless to say, the governor is not from the Agya clan. I look forward to doing this, Jenny. That girl of yours has to get out of here."

"Do you think she will be at the cafe tomorrow? What if she is not?" asked Jenny.

"If not tomorrow, we will do it the next day. You have little other choice. There is the bodyguard. She will have to try to escape on her own. But she has to know you are here and where she should go. You could try to kidnap her in the middle of the night, but the bodyguard could be trouble for you. He looks to be a professional."

Lizbeth entered the cafe at 11 the next morning. There was no sign of Sisi Akala. Lizbeth saw some people she knew and managed to stay there until 2 PM. Sisi had not come to the cafe that day.

"We will do it again tomorrow," said Lizbeth as she entered the house in mid-afternoon. "I must go to the center now. I will be back this evening."

"This is unbearable," said Jenny to Tim and Seydou who had nothing to do. They were stuck in the Anang house. Going out and showing themselves would not be a smart move. Isaac and Seydou ended up playing chess the whole afternoon. Tim found a book on African novelists that included summaries of their work.

Where are they? I know they're here. Korafa drove to the same spot Jenny and her men had been at the previous day to observe the Akala home. Nothing going on here. No Land Rover in sight that met the description of the source at the hotel in Bamako. It was an old model, he thought. Not many of those around anymore. The man's thoughts wandered as he observed the quiet compound below. After a time, he went to the cafe at the bottom of the hill. He sat down and tried to make out who would be the owner. He quickly sided on the man with the big white apron behind the bar. He switched to the bar and within a few minutes had the attention of the man. "I am looking for a colleague. Big muscular fellow with a shaved head who is looking after a young girl here in Yendi. He's a bodyguard of sort. His charge is a young lady who lives in the compound over the hill."

"Oh, you mean the young Akala girl. Her father died earlier this year. He was the area's veterinarian. She comes in here almost every day for a cola and to listen to music. Stays around for awhile. Yeah, the bodyguard is an imposing man. Looks to be a tough one. I know the family. They have strict controls on the girl but they are a good family. They let her come here. There is no alcohol served. We are Muslim. What do you want to know? Who are you?" Suddenly, the bar owner was the one asking the questions.

"I am an old friend of the man looking after her. We served together once. I will come back tomorrow. No rush in finding him. I can wait. Thank you."

"If he comes in, can I tell him someone, an old colleague is looking for him and will be here tomorrow?" asked the burly cafe owner.

"No, please don't. I would like to surprise him."

Lizbeth entered the cafe the next day. There was Sisi, sitting at a table in the corner. The bodyguard was not in sight. Lizbeth quickly went over to the girl, put her index finger to her mouth and gave Sisi the note. While Sisi was reading it, Lizbeth turned and finally saw what she was certain was Sisi's bodyguard talking to the owner. Lizbeth turned to the girl, put her finger again to her mouth, and took back the note. Sisi's eyes were wide, filled as much with terror as with excitement. Lizbeth asked with her eyes and a tilt of her head if she would do what the note said. The girl made a quick nod, then scanned the room to see where the bodyguard was. He was still in conversation with the owner. Lizbeth turned and left the cafe.

"She's terrified, Jenny. But she will do it. I saw it in her eyes," said Lizbeth after entering the house and finding everyone in anticipation of what she would say.

Korafa watched the cafe entrance from a vantage point behind some trees to see if Kuma and his charge would enter or leave. He had to know what she looked like. But primarily he had to be certain she was really there in Yendi. The cafe owner had said the day before he had not seen either of them for three days. A few minutes later, Wilson Kuma and a tall young girl emerged from the cafe and got into the Toyota Pick-up. She's here. That means Jenny is most certainly still here. She won't go back without the girl. They haven't gotten to her yet. I will watch the compound. Somebody will have to enter or leave for the girl to be taken away. One or the other. I will wait.

Wilson Kuma thought it strange. What the cafe owner had told him. Wanted it to be a surprise, he said. Has to be Korafa. Why is he here?

Sisi rose, got dressed in jeans, a t-shirt and a sweater. She kept the light off, went to the door and opened it a crack to see if any lights were on. None were. Not a sound anywhere. She tiptoed back to the window of her room, opened it wide, and crawled out, dropping ten feet to the ground. She crept along slowly away from the rooms where her grandmother and bodyguard were sleeping. She went up to the crest of the small hill off to the right, then over the top and crawled slowly down to the gully, the road and the vehicle waiting for her, out of site and earshot of the house.

Ahah. Things are happening, finally. Korafa heard the start of the engine off to the left and down the hill. Land Rover. Only they make that sound. He could make out the silhouette of the person moving through the bushes along the bed of the little stream in the direction of where the sound of the engine was coming from. He followed the silhouette, then saw the vehicle. It backed up slowly, turned around, then made its way to the main road a few hundred meters away. It's happening. Here we go. Lady, you are not going to survive this. Fifteen years. Fifteen long years.

The girl looked at the woman next to her. Their eyes fixed on each other, both with tears welling. "Mother," whispered the girl. "Sisi. My God. We're here. So long...." They embraced for a long moment while Seydou was proceeding down the road with the lights off. "Momma, we must hurry," said Sisi. "That man they had for me is a brute. He will come after us." Accelerating after leaving town, Seydou said for everyone, "I think somebody is after us. We are being followed. The same headlights have been following us through town and now on the highway. I will have to go off track, near where we found the road when coming in. We will see if he follows. It is still a long way to get there."

Korafa was surprised by the speed of the Land Rover. He had assumed he would be able to overtake it easily once on the highway. He could not know that Seydou Touré was a master mechanic and had worked on the old vehicle to give it 50% more horsepower, roughly the same increase in top speed and an enhanced suspension. He could not catch up. The Land Rover remained well ahead of him.

After over an hour and a hundred kilometers of going at top speed with the vehicle behind them struggling to keep up, Seydou turned off into the bush. He made his way through the rough terrain. He was certain he could outmaneuver the pursuer, whoever he was, and could add still more distance between them. Who was it? It couldn't be the bodyguard. He did not have enough time to react and get to a vehicle, even if he had noticed almost immediately that Sisi was no longer in the house. Who was it? He looked in the rear view mirror. The vehicle had followed them.

Seydou Touré drove at near breakneck speed through the bush, going around trees, around dips in the ground and over and around small hills. He had turned on his lights and so had the vehicle in pursuit. Ten or so kilometers into the terrain, Seydou remembered a steep river bank they had to climb on the way in. He turned off the lights and proceeded slowly forward to find the river bank, saw that it was not far ahead, then turned left just before the edge to find the dip that he had found on their way in three mornings before. They had used it to cross the stream and regain the terrain. Seydou said to his passengers as they went down the slope and crossed the river, "If he keeps going straight, he will go over the edge."

After crossing the stream, Seydou turned right, went a hundred meters, then turned left into the bush terrain to be in line with the track taken on the other side and turned his lights on again.

All right. There they are. Time to catch up. Korafa accelerated - he could see the lights of the Land Rover once again in the distance. He had to get closer. He was going as fast as he could. He looked down to the left as he sped by - tire tracks going off. Uh oh...He realized at that second what was going to happen but it was too late. The Land Cruiser went over the edge at high speed, tumbled end over end and came to rest on its crushed roof in a foot of water. By the time a herder found the vehicle in the river a day and a half later, Mustafa Korafa had been dead for over 24 hours.

Wilson Kuma rose in his bed, looked at his watch. 5:15. He got up, left the room and crossed the central living area. The door to the girl's room was open. He looked in and saw the wide open window. She was gone. He ran outside, found footprints leading to the gully and the line of trees along the stream.

Korafa. He came to get her. That's why he was here. Revenge against the woman. Revenge against the Akalas. Will he kill her? What else will he do? Have to call the police. Can't deal with this on my own. Madame will be screaming for my head.

A man in the village told the police later that morning he had seen a black Toyota Land Cruiser under some trees on the crest of the hill overlooking the Akala compound the previous evening as he walked to his cousin's house. Korafa's truck, thought Kuma. It WAS him. There was no sign of the vehicle anywhere in Yendi. No one else saw a vehicle of the same description either moving through or on the roads leading from the town.

The police arrived at the site where the herder had found the Land Cruiser and Mustafa Korafa lying dead beneath it. There was no sign of the girl or any evidence there had been another person in the vehicle. The police did find tire tracks leading from the other side of the stream and managed to follow them to the unmarked border area another hundred kilometers away. They contacted the Burkina Faso border police. Both police forces issued alerts for their airports and road border crossings to look out for a young light skinned girl who would probably be travelling with someone. No further description could be provided.

Madame Akala was furious with Kuma. She was sure of who took the girl and it was not Mustafa Korafa. Kuma was all wrong. The police believed Kuma, however. He was one of them. He was aware Korafa had been in Yendi the day before and knew all about a motive that the man had. He was certain it was Korafa. But Madame was sure of who did it and it was not him. It Jenny had come to Ghana and had retrieved her daughter. Finding Korafa dead in the bush and no sign of Sisi with him only confirmed such to Madame. Although now in disfavor with the government and the local authorities, she exhorted the police to have the borders watched and initiate serious efforts to get her granddaughter back. A Ghanaian citizen had been kidnapped by an American. The government had to do something about it. She was furious the police had wasted time looking for Korafa. Kidnapping a citizen of the country even if it was by the person's mother could not go unchallenged.

With the discovery of Korafa and no sign the girl had been with him, the police moved to issue pictures of Sisi Akala to their foreign intelligence colleagues. They asked them to watch for the girl who would be accompanied by a white woman and perhaps others at the airports of Accra, Ouagadougou, Bamako and Lomé to the east. All the border crossings leading out of Ghana were provided descriptions and orders to detain. A senior police officer who had a debt to honor to an old friend who had saved his life once, went through the motions but ensured that the activities of his officers would be too little too late. No one thought of asking the Russians, who would have, in any case, expressed ignorance of it all.

"I haven't known you, Mother. It is going to take some time," said Sisi in the Land Rover as they drove through Burkina Faso. "This is all very disturbing. I have no idea of what I am going to. I have never been out of Ghana."

"My dear, I realize all that," replied Jenny. "But I think you will like where we are going to. I will make sure you are as happy as I can, Sisi. I have waited fifteen years for the opportunity to make you happy. I will not mess it up. You will have Efe and all your cousins to help you."

Sisi looked at Jenny who was sitting next to her and put her head on her mother's shoulder. "You used to do this when you were little," said Jenny. "You would get up on the cushions on the sofa and put your head on my shoulder."

The girl was quiet for the next hour as she closed her eyes, took some deep breaths giving evidence of the tension she had felt since the previous afternoon, and before. She dozed off with her head resting on her mother's shoulder and her legs curled up on the seat.

"Where are we? Are we really free?" she asked as she awoke. Before getting an answer, she continued, "I cannot bear to have to deal with Kuma, or with Grandmama, if we are caught."

"We will not be free for some time yet, Sisi, but I don't think you have much to worry about," said Tim. "We have two other borders to cross. Things could get complicated, but the U.S. authorities are prepared to intervene if there is trouble."

Seydou and Tim alternated driving. They crossed virtually the entire length of Burkina Faso and entered Mali during the night. Brian joined them north of Bamako. The eleven-hour run to Dakar was without incident other than the long, bumpy ride. There, they stayed in the U.S. Embassy until their flight to Paris and then on to New York.

We did it, I have them back, she thought, as the plane rumbled down the runway.

Epilogue

They spent hours talking about the lives they had had during their long separation. The girls read every one of the copies of the letters their mother had sent them over the years.

Sisi never heard from the man she was to marry. Africa was behind her. Neither she or Efe ever heard from their grandmother again.

Wilson Kuma, banned from the Akala house, met with the chief of staff of the President and told him what he had learned of the activities of Madame Akala. The corruption, the buying of votes, bribes to gain construction contracts, her hiring a man to eliminate a politician.

With her long-serving driver, Grandmother Akala crossed the Togo border late one night, drove to Lomé, and took a flight to Kampala, Uganda, never to return. She did not have the opportunity to enjoy her exile for very long. She died of a stroke a year later, in the midst of attempts of the government of Ghana to extradite her to face multiple charges of corruption and conspiracy to commit murder.

Jay Peterson stayed in touch with Jenny after her move with the girls to Boston. He had realized years before that he was attracted to her. He went to Boston as often as he could. At one of the lunches they had, Jenny asked him a question. "Jay, you follow New York politics and all that. Whatever happened to that guy who harassed me a few years ago, Richard Keyes, the head of protocol for the city back then?"

"He lost the job. A young girl working at the city complained about being harassed. There was an investigation. She was not alone. He had to resign. He left for Trinidad and nobody, as far as I know, has heard from him since."

Jay had a question of his own. "What ever happened to that secret service guy who was after you? A real number. Stopped me on the road after I had met you. His men roughed me up a couple nights later."

"I don't know. The last I heard of him was when he was deported back to Ghana from here after he tried to threaten me," replied Jenny. "Over five years ago. He disappeared for me after that."

At another one of Jay's visits that year, after dinner at one of Boston's finest, she asked him if he would like to stay over. He said yes. He wondered later how it had taken so long to happen. Within a few weeks, Jay Peterson, upon his request, was transferred to Boston as bureau chief of NewsMag Media.

A few years later, a new government was elected in Ghana. The appointed foreign affairs minister was Kwasi Kobena, Jenny Sutton's first contact at Ghana's New York UN mission. Kobena remembered the tall, distressed American woman who had come to see him with her story. He had always felt bad that he could not help her. He had his people track her down. It was not for punishment or harassment or for anything to do with the exit of her children from the country years before. It was to be for something entirely different. Kobena had been made aware of the extent of her difficulties in getting access to her children over the years by an old friend in Tamale, Lizbeth Anang, who he ran into at a post-election reception in Yende. Soon, an invitation was received by Jenny at her office in Boston from a Ghanaian diplomat. It was an invitation from Minister Kwasi Kobena - "My God, Kwasi from the UN Mission, so long ago" Jenny said to herself - to attend the dedication of a new school for girls in Yendi. The invitation included an open return ticket from Boston to Accra. The diplomat assured Jenny that the intent of the Minister was honorable and that she could certainly be accompanied by a representative of the U.S. Embassy if she wished. Jenny was apprehensive but accepted the invitation and travelled to Accra and on to Yendi with Jay a few weeks later.

At the ceremony with the Minister along with Lizbeth and the local teacher who had helped Jenny plan another school there almost twenty years before, as well as more than one hundred other people, the school plaque was unveiled with its new name. The Jenny School. The lady who had been shunned by the village nearly two decades before and had expended so many years and tears in her odyssey, was overwhelmed. She did not know what to say. The guests began to clap, and clap and clap. The slow, rhythmic clap with everyone smiling and swaying seemed to last forever. The head of the village asked for quiet and spoke. "Mrs. Sutton, *Ye re kose. Akoaba ekyir.* We are sorry. Welcome back."

Tom Creary

www.tomcreary.com

www.ingramcontent.com/pod-product-compliance
Lightning Source LLC
Chambersburg PA
CBHW071138260626
47162CB00003B/836